GW00454963

PENGUI
OUT OF

Harsha Bhogle is widely recognized as the face and the voice of Indian cricket. He brings to his profession an unusual set of gifts that give him a distinct identity in the cricket world. Harsha is many things: a chemical engineer who graduated from India's number one business school IIM Ahmedabad, an advertising executive, an iconic television presenter who spawned a TV reality show called *Hunt for Harsha* (*Harsha ki Khoj*), a commentator who is popular across cultures, a sensitive talk show host, a corporate motivational speaker (an enterprise he runs with his wife Anita), and a writer with a great feel for the game and its actors. A recipient of numerous awards, he was voted the 'most favourite cricket commentator' in a worldwide poll of readers of Cricinfo.com in 2008. One of his proudest possessions is a photograph of a group of spectators in Pakistan holding a banner that says 'Harsha Bhogle fan club'.

Harsha has been the face of ESPN in India since the day they went on air in 1995, and presents cricket—and, in an interesting diversion, the football World Cup in 2006—for ESPN Star Sports. He has worked on all the major radio stations in the cricketing world as well, with a special affinity for Australia, which he first visited in 1991-92, where he was dubbed the 'sexiest voice on radio'. He is close to achieving the double of working on 100 Tests and 400 one-day internationals, the first of which was in 1983.

Originally from Hyderabad, and still enamoured of the flavour of the city, Harsha lives in Mumbai in a close-knit family with his wife Anita (an IIM Ahmedabad alumna) and sons Chinmay and Satchit.

PRAISE FOR *OUT OF THE BOX*

'Harsha's writing reflects his flair for the written word combined with a knowledge and love of the game.'—Rahul Dravid

'Harsha remains a bright, engaging voice in an often contentious world. He writes as he lives, cheerfully, intelligently, tolerant of man's foibles but not the world's decay. Like all countries, India relies on its honest broker to tell it the truth. Harsha does so with unfailing humour and humility.'—Peter Roebuck

OUT OF THE BOX

WATCHING THE GAME
WE LOVE

Harsha Bhogle

INTRODUCTION BY
Sachin Tendulkar

Revised Edition

THE
EXPRESS
GROUP

PENGUIN BOOKS

PENGUIN BOOKS

Published by the Penguin Group

Penguin Books India Pvt. Ltd, 11 Community Centre, Panchsheel Park,
New Delhi 110 017, India
Penguin Group (USA) Inc., 375 Hudson Street, New York, New York 10014, USA
Penguin Group (Canada), 90 Eglinton Avenue East, Suite 700, Toronto,
Ontario, M4P 2Y3, Canada (a division of Pearson Penguin Canada Inc.)
Penguin Books Ltd, 80 Strand, London WC2R 0RL, England
Penguin Ireland, 25 St Stephen's Green, Dublin 2, Ireland
(a division of Penguin Books Ltd)
Penguin Group (Australia), 250 Camberwell Road, Camberwell,
Victoria 3124, Australia (a division of Pearson Australia Group Pty Ltd)
Penguin Group (NZ), 67 Apollo Drive, Rosedale, Auckland 0632,
New Zealand (a division of Pearson New Zealand Ltd)
Penguin Group (South Africa) (Pty) Ltd, 24 Sturdee Avenue, Rosebank,
Johannesburg 2196, South Africa

Penguin Books Ltd, Registered Offices: 80 Strand, London WC2R 0RL, England

First published in Viking by Penguin Books India 2009
This revised and updated edition published in Penguin Books 2011

Copyright © Harsha Bhogle 2009, 2011

All rights reserved

10 9 8 7 6 5 4 3 2 1

ISBN 9780143417507

The views and opinions expressed in this book are the author's own and the facts are as
reported by him which have been verified to the extent possible, and the publishers are
not in any way liable for the same.

Cover photograph by Neeraj Priyadarshi, *Indian Express*

Typeset in Sabon Roman by SÜRYA, New Delhi
Printed at Chaman Offset Printers, Delhi

I have been fortunate to have met some remarkable people but my hero came into my life very early. My elder brother Bhau—I could never call him Srinivas—told me, and demonstrated with his own actions, the need to take the right path and the power of honesty.

This one is for him, my biggest hero.

CONTENTS

ODIs

TESTS

CRICKETING GREATS

RULES, REGULATIONS, INFRASTRUCTURE

FOREWORD

Shekhar Gupta

If on TV his words make you see what's not on the screen, in writing he takes you way beyond what he already told you from the commentary box. It's an ability few individuals can match in the Indian media, that of being able to tell the story as it unfolds on camera so coherently, and then taking it forward in print. This is what makes Harsha Bhogle so unique. And this is the reason he has been able to prosper in a business increasingly dominated by former players. In fact, he is today the only 'pure' professional in the commentary box, though Harsha would indignantly remind you of the days he played competitive cricket in Hyderabad.

India has had a fairly healthy tradition of talented commentators, some of whom were loved by millions for their ability to describe the game and some for their colourful nature or idiosyncracies. But post-live TV, Harsha is a star in his own right. To that extent he is an original and, until now, the only one.

All great games inspire great prose, more so cricket, with its lazy elegance. The game has changed much, so has its pace, but Harsha still brings an old-world charm to cricket writing, describing a moment with the excitement and passion it deserves. Harsha can tell you the story of a game with remarkable equanimity and partisan detachment, irrespective of whether India is winning or losing, whether the cricketer he loves is scoring a hundred or living through one more failure.

However, make no mistakes; behind that impregnable professional persona on camera, Harsha is deeply partisan. He loves the game of cricket, but he also loves his team. And they love and trust him as well.

That is why Harsha's columns have brought so much value to the *Indian Express* sports pages. That is also the reason this collection is such a fine addition to our bookshelves, particularly so in a country with so few quality books on sports.

INTRODUCTION

Sachin Tendulkar

'In a gentle way, you can shake the world'
—*Mohandas Karamchand Gandhi*

The first time I met Harsha was when he interviewed me for a sports magazine when I was fourteen. I vividly remember that evening. We sat on one of the pitches in Shivaji Park and the interview slowly transformed into a larger discussion on cricket. Having seen Harsha grow over the years as a commentator and presenter, I am in high spirits as I write this introduction.

Cricket as a sport is a passion for millions in our country and here is an individual who chose to be different to the extent that he envisioned a career path which was unknown to many even a few years ago.

Harsha epitomizes what you can achieve if you really put your heart and soul into a cause. Despite his self-confessed dreams of playing for India not materializing, he has still managed to stay connected to the game and contribute substantially over the years to our understanding of cricket.

When you meet Harsha, first things you notice are his sense of humour and his keen eye for detail—not to mention his infectious laughter. On a more serious note, I have come to realize that speaking to him sometimes opens up completely different perspectives in addition to the ones I already have. He has a high cricketing acumen, which has not only helped him carve a niche identity, but also sustain himself in the television commentary space amongst legends of the game.

I'm sure this book will not only inspire readers to chase their own dreams but also empower them with the best practices on how to lead the field and become world-class in their professional life.

Wishing him lots of luck,

Sachin Tendulkar

PREFACE

The box has been my identity and my boundary. It has given me opportunities I could not have dreamed of, introduced me to some lovely people and allowed me to be part of some beautiful moments, but more than anything else it has allowed me to enter · people's houses and, sometimes, become friends with them.

Television can be a very powerful medium, but it can also be limiting. The escalation of television rights means commercial intrusion is inevitable. You have to be precise, a quick jab with a word or a comment, and out before the break. You can't paint a picture with someone waiting to take the brush away. That is the reality of modern television, and commentators must adapt.

But with a laptop in front of you, and an empty screen, you can reflect, ponder aloud over issues, fret over a word, erase it, dab a little more colour here, a little detail there and present a finished product that is yours, and yours alone. While television rewards spontaneity, the written word demands weightiness. It is a completely different genre but one that is crippled by insensitivity to words.

Words are a writer's wand and his weapon. They evoke feelings and paint pictures for the reader. They must be respected. Not everyone can write like Peter Roebuck or Rohit Brijnath, but, even in our limited sphere, we must use words carefully, not toss them around. Good cricketers we write about don't offer just any shot to a ball. So too must cricket writers pick words they believe are most appropriate. Peter once told me of the twin loves of his life: cricket and the English language. They work well together, certainly in our game which lends itself to fine writing.

Writing a weekly column can present a different challenge. True, you have the entire week to reflect on what happens, but inevitably, there is a rush towards the end. Sometimes the defining moment comes on a Monday, too early for a Thursday deadline, and so passes you by. At others it comes late on Thursday evening and you have to appear weighty and yet spontaneous. But that is part of the challenge for the columnist and overall it can be fun and rewarding because you have an address and people know where to visit you.

I have been very happy with my address at the *Indian Express*. They have been good to me, have honoured my only request which was not to edit my pieces, because then they wouldn't be mine any more. And now they do me the honour of putting together a selection from all that I have written for them into this anthology. It means a lot to me. Being in cricket has been a mighty blessing, this makes it sweeter.

Over the years some of what I have written is still relevant, some of it has withered with time. So do look upon this book as a collection of snapshots, some fresh, some dated, hopefully pleasantly. You cannot always cater to the immediate and aspire for posterity.

I'd like to thank Shekhar Gupta for this. He called me some years ago, we agreed in the first couple of minutes on the column, and talked cricket for a long time after that.

His sports editors have since become friends. First the football-loving, jovial Jayaditya Gupta, followed by Ajay Shankar, who knows all that is happening in Indian cricket, and then Kunal Pradhan, who brings a fine style to his own writing.

And I would like to thank Sachin Tendulkar. He has given me so much pleasure over the years and not once has he behaved like the massive star he is. And now he has honoured me deeply by writing an introduction to this book.

I hope cricket grows stronger because it has defined our existence, certainly mine, for so many years, whether in the box or out of it.

T20s

20–20 VISION IS THE WAY AHEAD

21 January 2005

Little sparks become raging fires; small gatherings become uncontrollable mobs; tiny trends acquire cult following. In each case the key is to spot things early; a good policeman would do that, so would a sharp equity investor. Mapping trends is the subject of a most interesting book by Malcolm Gladwell, appropriately called *The Tipping Point*, the point at which a movement becomes unstoppable. Had Gladwell been a student of contemporary cricket, he would have added another case study to his impressive collection: 20–20 cricket.

Like with most innovations, 20–20 cricket is torn between the traditionalists and the early adopters. Being a mere marketing issue, and not a messy matter of a church or a temple, the marketing man will win, assuming of course that he has the desire to do so. 20–20 will be here to stay: frenetic action, instant gratification; it is a product of the times. It cannot be stopped.

How interesting it is that the 50-over game is now

This was one of the first articles to be written on the phenomenon called Twenty20 cricket (then known as 20–20 cricket).

3

throwing up traditionalists, for its own birth lay in revolution, its progress a stinging riposte to antique thought. As the original revolutionaries grow middle-aged they probably hold on to their own symbols of revolt: Che Guevara maybe, Jim Morrison maybe, Amitabh Bachchan and 50-over cricket with coloured clothing.

But 20–20 need not replace 50-over cricket, for life, most often, is not about substitution but addition. T-shirts can live with ties, sneakers with fine leather. And so the happy coexistence of Test cricket and one-day cricket can get happier with the arrival of 20–20. The customer will have a wider range to choose from.

Like rock and roll, reggae and rap, Rafi, Rahman and remix, so too Test cricket, one-day cricket and 20–20. That is how it must be. The customer must be king and he will choose, for the objective of sport is to entertain.

I actually believe 20–20 cricket will rejuvenate 50-over cricket in much the manner the limited-overs international did with Test cricket. For some time now one-day cricket has carried a tired look to it: a good hotel with old carpets. Too many games have been predictable; the middle overs follow a formula, one surface is like another.

You still get close games but their definition has changed. Viewers and players alike are better educated, more discerning. A 10-run margin is a pretty big win now and 50 overs is too long for mediocre teams to achieve parity with good ones; and it is parity which is what makes for a good contest.

So do we dilute skills even more, throw the bowler out of the game, reduce our sport to a public flogging of ball by bat? No, we create a new category, find a breed of players who can perform instantly. Just as cinema has the long and dramatic *Titanic*, the irreverent display of reality in *Fahrenheit 9/11* and the glossy 30-second commercial, so too must cricket present a basket of offerings to its faithful.

It will probably redefine standards of good and average as well. Till ten years ago, conceding around 30 runs in 10 overs was very good, under 40 was very acceptable. We have now come to accept that anything under 50 runs from a 10-over spell is pretty decent given the kind of pitches, quality of bats and sophistication of hitting. But 5 an over in Test cricket is poor, 4 an over means a bowler hasn't had a great day. So too with 20–20, where 7 an over will probably become a benchmark, 8 an over the first target for a batting side.

India will have to join in, though there will be debate on whether or not we need it, given that cricket has no competition. But as marketing men will tell you the next rival must come from within, the flanking product must be yours. And India will have to adapt quickly because 20–20 will be the athlete's game. And athleticism hasn't always been our strong point.

Coaches will have to redefine themselves and television will have to rise to the occasion. Those haven't been strong points recently in India either.

It will give sponsors who find themselves priced out of one-day cricket a new vehicle; it will draw the marginal followers in. It will add to the entertainment. It is time to feel the fresh breeze blowing. If we don't, it will just move on and leave us behind.

YOUR GUIDE TO WATCHING TWENTY20: RISK REDEFINED, OLD IS BURIED

14 September 2007

We are experiencing the birth of a new baby and have no mother or mother-in-law, or indeed midwife, to tell us what is right and what isn't. There are no theories and no laws, not yet; there are only hypotheses and, much like chemists before the periodic table, even the experts are hitting in the dark a little bit. But what I am convinced about is that we are seeing the beginning of a revolution. In times to come, those of us fortunate enough to be around here will say 'I was there'.

The one defining factor, indeed the biggest factor, is that a team has 10 wickets in hand over a shorter period. Everything else, the shot making, the running between wickets, even the bowling, derives from this.

That changes definitions of risk as we know them and, in doing so, this game will create its own grammar. And I just have a feeling that most early theories will get buried.

This article was written soon after the beginning of the first ICC Twenty20 World Cup in South Africa on 11 September 2007.

We are all talking about this being a batsman's game. But don't forget that the batsmen are expected to go hell for leather, to hit the ball a bus-stop away. The pressure is on them to deliver and, so, there is always an opportunity for a calm bowler and a calm captain.

Indeed, my view is that in this seemingly frenetic 200-miles-an hour sport, the calmest mind will prevail. Just as it probably is in Formula One. The moment a batsman blocks, or is forced to block two balls, the pressure on him mounts. In a batsman's game, the pressure is on the batsman just as, in a Shah Rukh Khan movie, the pressure is on Shah Rukh.

This is where having ten wickets will come in handy. The price on a wicket diminishes in direct proportion to the number of overs. The greater the number of overs, the higher the value of the wicket; correspondingly, the fewer the number of overs, the greater risk you can take, and so batsmen can play the desperate shot quite early. That is the opportunity for the bowler, but I also suspect something else is going to happen.

As batsmen take chances, they will discover that some of them aren't as risky as earlier perceived. In Test cricket, for example, hitting in the air was frowned upon earlier for fear that you might get caught. In recent years, batsmen have discovered that hitting through the line and over the top isn't as dangerous as was thought. That was due to 50-over cricket.

Now, I believe Twenty20s will induce a similar change in perception and make 50-over cricket faster. Just to give you an example, batsmen tend to check their shot if they find they have been deceived by a slower ball. Here, they might discover that if they keep going, there might be a decent percentage of safety.

And the definition of a good bowler will change. When

Joel Garner was bowling in limited-overs cricket, 3.5 an over was routine. Now we believe that anything under 5 an over on most days is good bowling. Here, bowlers will say that under 30 runs in 4 overs is very good. In fact they may well assess themselves on a ball-by-ball basis and regard a ball not scored off as a little victory in itself.

Make no mistake—this is a game for the six-hitter. And for the inventive batsman. If 10 an over becomes a good score and 8 an over the minimum, the well-placed and briskly run two will diminish in value. The single won't be as critical either; a bit like punctuation really, you need it but not always!

Remember there are no middle overs in this game. It is not a slog fest, the good cricket shot will still have value, but the urgency never ceases because, again, you have 10 wickets to lose over 20 overs.

So how do we enjoy Twenty20 cricket? By not equating it to anything we already know. We enjoy a pani-puri without lamenting the absence of a slow-cooked Hyderabadi biryani. Just as there is room on the palate and in the stomach for both, so too with Twenty20 and 50-over and Test cricket.

Those who say 'this is not cricket' and splutter over their coffee can pull out their manual typewriter, search for photographic film and call in the pigeons to send messages. Just enjoy it for what it is. Sometimes it is good to put the jacket and tie aside and slip on a round-neck tee.

MINIMIZE THE CULT OF
THE INDIVIDUAL

28 September 2007

There was much joy, hype, finger-pointing and attention-seeking, neither of which was unexpected, as India's cricketers returned to Mumbai. As Kipling had hoped, we treat those two impostors, triumph and disaster, the same: with melodrama! And so people waited in the rain, in stifling humidity, in crowds with not an inch to move—and they could not have been too different from the people who abused and heckled the cricketers six months ago.*
Maybe our much-abused movies, with no subtle shades of character, with only black or white, know India better than the others!

The awards were welcome for this is a genuinely outstanding achievement but I'm a little uncomfortable

The Indian cricket team won the first ICC Twenty20 World Cup on 27 September 2007 at the Wanderers, defeating Pakistan in the final.

*After India crashed out of the World Cup in the Caribbean in the first stage, in the 50-over version of the game.

with singling out individuals within a team for greater honour. Good teams seek to minimize, indeed to destroy, the cult of the individual. It has been a problem with our cricket and it is a touch dangerous to fan these fires. And you have to have sympathy for our hockey players who work as hard and dream as vividly as our cricketers. But they play a sport that is run by callous, indifferent people and so cricket and hockey are at different levels on the remuneration ladder. A young ambitious chef straight out of catering college doesn't get paid the same as a young ambitious investment banker. But while private enterprise can be market driven, governments cannot differentiate between one and the other. Now if only we could confiscate hockey from the current regime, we might have happier tales to narrate!

Sympathy is a word that has often been used with Misbah-ul-Huq, a fine player who twice brought Pakistan to the brink of victory. He even picked a good shot but found Joginder Sharma didn't have the pace on the ball to take it beyond the edge of the circle. Misbah will know, more than anyone in world sport at the moment, that the ability to finish games separates the great players from the good. A lot of teams can bring a ball to within three yards of the goal but it requires a great striker to put it at the back of the net. Strikers are valued because they finish moves, great golfers are those that play the eighteenth as well as the previous seventeen, even the boxer who dominates a bout needs a finishing punch. Misbah didn't have it.

It was good to see though that in the end good bowlers took wickets and good batsmen scored runs. In course of time, this game will evolve its own grammar but whatever it turns out to be, it will not be bereft of skill. As long as a bowler has a chance of getting a batsman out, and the game isn't tinkered with too much to prevent that from happening, you will have to be skilful to play it at the highest level. Remember batsmen are taking chances and that always represents hope for the bowler and one of the happiest conclusions of this tournament is that taking wickets counts. If Pakistan had been six down instead of nine, they would have had a better chance of winning it.

However, I dread the day they start bringing the boundary ropes in and making flatter pitches. A six must still represent an achievement and if batsmen hit it at will, it makes the game boring. The only match at the Twenty20 World Cup that left me cold was Sri Lanka vs Kenya. I switched off because there was no contest. A little bit in the pitch for the bowlers and a boundary rope far enough to allow a batsman to be caught and you really have everything you need.

I must confess to being a little distressed at the barbs being directed at Tendulkar, Ganguly and Dravid for not appearing at the felicitation. They couldn't have and they did well not to because it wasn't their moment. Dhoni has said that they called him, there were messages of congratulations and that is about all there should be. In the search for a good story we cannot cross the boundaries of grace and indeed, of truth. Far too often these days the truth is becoming too large, too inconvenient, a burden to carry. Quotes are tampered with, conclusions need not derive from facts. And news anchors routinely shout down guests who dare to have an opinion different from the one that the channel seeks to propagate.

EXCELLENCE IS THE WAY TO MAKE PROFITS IN IPL

8 February 2008

There are many reasons why I believe the IPL could be the best thing to happen to Indian cricket. The need has often been stated but now there is a path that is visible; amidst the jungle, a trail has emerged and we must follow it with hope. I do not know if there are speedbreakers on the way but what I do know is that it is the only option ahead at the moment.

In this column I have often spoken of my dream; that Indian cricket will have parents who will nurture it. At the moment Indian cricket is the poor little rich kid and relatives with different shades of character are befriending it hoping to get a slice of the pie. They want to see the kid get richer, not necessarily better. Being rich and being good are not always synonymous. Indian cricket needs nurturing but how does a flagrantly commercial proposition achieve this end?

Quite simply because, in being selfish, you sometimes

This piece was written just before the player auctions for the first season of the Indian Premier League (IPL).

12

find the right approach. Return on investment is very often a good path towards excellence. When being good is the only way to make profits, you are forced to be good and that is at the heart of all successful commercial enterprise. Bidders have paid large amounts of money to own franchises and since they are not in the business of losing money, they will try and produce the best possible teams. To them this is merely a new line of business. Reliance built world-class petrochemical complexes, GMR are building fine airports; in either case excellence is the way to profits. I believe it will be the same with the cricket teams they own.

And so, just as they pick the right project managers and sales executives, they will pick the right players and instil in them the need to play to a certain standard. As employees get sacked for non-performance, players will too and in course of time they will realize that you don't play this game merely to be in the team but to win. Team players will be rewarded; in football the flamboyant striker gets a great deal but so does the solid mid-fielder who may not sell T-shirts but who breaks down opposition attacks.

Occasionally, just as the personnel manager's nephew might get an out-of-turn interview, so will a player who knows the right people, but in the harsh world of performance and results, only the best will stay. Selectors will be accountable, so will coaches.

Development in cricket and in younger, newer players will become an investment. I can see franchisees picking young kids and putting them on long-term contracts; maybe not even playing them for a couple of years till they are ready but ensuring that when they are, they are available only to those franchisees. One of the greatest problems in our cricket is the talent we lose in the age group 16–18 because of selectors who are not accountable and occasionally lured towards more personal objectives.

The other major issue is, rightly, the need for education and a job. I can already see franchisees addressing both issues; send a sixteen-year-old to school by day and get him to train and play cricket by evening. If he makes it, the world is his oyster, else he has a qualification that the franchisee can find useful for employment elsewhere.

But for that to happen a franchisee must have more to do than a mere month and a half of 20-overs cricket. I believe the BCCI should begin a divestment process where all cricket is slowly moved towards private ownership. A Reliance or a Kingfisher should have three teams; a 20-over team, a 50-over team and a four-day team. The top franchise of the year will be the one that produces the best results over all three forms. Two years is a good enough time to wait and see how the franchise model works and to iron out problems that will inevitably arise. Then we must go the whole hog.

We won't because there are too many vested interests. Power without accountability is a potent drug and state associations who manage the dreaded vote will dig in their heels. But even here a solution can present itself. The experience with public sector units now managed by the private sector is that the moment there is a reward for performance everybody delivers. The person who wouldn't look up as he sat on files gets a move on. Even state associations under private ownership will deliver.

The selectors will then only have to pick from the best that have already been picked. The job of finding talent will already have been effectively outsourced and we won't need to have this stupid, self-defeating situation of twenty-seven first-class teams. Under a franchisee system where the best talent will be sourced wherever it is from, fifteen teams will do just fine.

We are on the threshold of something very big. All it

needs is a touch of statesmanship and an overriding love of Indian cricket. The poor little rich kid can become a strapping, wise young man. The next two years can lay the foundation for the next fifty.

ARRANGED MARRIAGES STILL WORK, THEY ARE STILL HONOURABLE

15 February 2008

The confusion in world cricket at the moment reminds me a bit of what happens immediately after the light turns green at a busy Mumbai traffic junction. Everybody is in a hurry to get ahead but some people haven't yet finished turning right from the earlier signal. People are veering left, getting exasperated at the auto-rickshaw and the ability of the driver to ignore curses hurled at him; a bus is blocking the next lane, everyone is honking, there is a lot of noise, the people ten cars behind are getting worked up fearing they may miss another signal. And yet it happens all the time. Four hundred yards later, equilibrium is reached, the chaos has sorted itself out, another path has been found and everybody moves on till the next traffic junction. You know what is going to happen and yet, you can't stop yourself getting annoyed, thinking you own the traffic and that, therefore, it must follow your needs.

India's eventful and controversial tour of Australia ended on 1 February 2008.

If you don't understand Mumbai's traffic you can't drive in it. If you are worked up and angry, you soon discover that the guy in the car next to you couldn't care less. And now, the cricket world is discovering that if they want a share of the riches that corporate India bestows onto Indian cricket, they need to learn to drive in India. At the moment they are getting exasperated, frustrated and angry, they are used to driving in their own lane, used to the predictability of giving way at a roundabout and can't fathom what to do with the spontaneity of Indian cricket.

They, Australia in particular, don't know what it is to dart into the next lane, ignore the look, and dart back. Australia have been leaders in world cricket and suddenly there is an unknown monster, the IPL, upon them. Australia have been leaders, at thought and at organization, and that combination has meant they have been leaders on the playing field as well. On both those counts, thought and organization, India have been closer to the bottom and it is only the ability to live in Brownian motion, in constant chaos (and the use of the word 'chaos' is not derogatory but descriptive) that has allowed India to have its occasional moment in the sun. Now Australia fear they are going to get a touch marginalized and so they are digging in, making sporadic attacks; some justified, some, like Tim May's suggestion that the IPL compensate cricket boards, laughable.

In course of time, the equivalent of the four hundred yards after a Mumbai traffic signal, there will be order again and people will know where they stand. But while that happens, people will do what they think right. However, they will have to co-exist, like the BMW does with the auto-rickshaw, and to be able to do that they must understand each other, appreciate that they need each other, that everybody has a right to be on the road, and that therefore, one is not necessarily more correct than the other.

The lesson from this year's tour of Australia is that world cricket needs India and Australia to understand each other and their cultures better. Hawkish, sensationalist stances don't help. India has the money, Australia play cricket better and harder than the others, the two need each other. Arranged marriages still work, they are still honourable.

And while on the topic of confusion, there is yet another that will soon confront the IPL, or more specifically the franchise owners. For years now, to the young man in Karol Bagh or Triplicane, Sachin Tendulkar scoring runs is something to revel about. Can they, in their minds, reconcile to the idea that a Tendulkar dismissal is a moment of celebration? That if Lee playing for Chennai gets Tendulkar playing for Mumbai out, they are supposed to cheer for Lee? Can they pray to their gods the previous evening that Tendulkar or Ganguly or Dravid gets out early? Can the kid in Bandra or Himayatnagar hope that Nel gets Dhoni or that Gilchrist smashes Sreesanth? And then, a month later, wish for the opposite?

After having spent years adoring cricketers who play for India, can they feel similarly about their city? I know it happens in football all the time but you don't have the dramatic one-on-one contests in football that you do in cricket. It will take time to get used to the idea of supporting two teams, for cricket has aroused nationalistic feelings like few other things have. Much has to happen still, those four hundred yards are going to take time to negotiate. But there will be equilibrium in the end.

LEAGUE OF THE UNKNOWNS

18 April 2008

By a delicious coincidence, India's latest blockbuster releases on a Friday. And like all releases, the hype has reached a crescendo, masking as it does the uncertainty in the producer's gut. Make no mistake, it is there. You can bank on your assets, minimize your risks and yet, there is always something left undone. And in the end, performance has to speak for itself. So let us get ready for the performances.

And yet, it would be unfair to compare the Indian Premier League to a Friday release where fortunes are made and lost in the first three days. This is more like a brand launch, to be assessed at the end of the season, for commitments are in place for much longer. Few brands get it right the first time; and when the horizon is ten years, the first year becomes a learning phase rather than a do-or-die shootout.

But for the first time, the eyes of the world will be on India. Will it have as much of an impact as Kerry Packer's World Series Cricket did? Will it be bigger? Thirty years

---

The first season of the Indian Premier League (IPL) started on Friday 18 April 2008.

19

from now, will Friday the 18th of April be seen as a defining moment in the history of the game? A lot of people are watching from the sidelines, waiting to see what happens before they make their first move.

In England the players will be seeing how much they have lost, and thereby strengthen their case for playing with the world's best.* There is no secret about which side they are on and there is fear that somebody in England will seize the moment and begin a breakaway league. It could work and it may not. It may not because there isn't the same amount of money and passion going around, but who is to stop a world league of Twenty20 led by the Indian Cricket League? England is the crucible at the moment and the administration has to act quickly. Either they set up their own league, or alter the season to accommodate the IPL, or risk losing players elsewhere. I believe we are not too far from a re-alignment of traditional cricket in England; certainly at least as far as a Twenty20 tournament is concerned.

The International Cricket Council (ICC) will be looking to see if the IPL merits a window in the calendar. The players think so and certainly the new chief executive† thinks so too. But you need to look beyond the first year. Currently we are looking at six weeks. If the IPL becomes what the franchise owners hope it will be, there will need to be more teams, more matches, longer seasons. That will be inevitable if this is a big hit in the first year because franchises will be looking for returns on investment and a longer season might benefit them.

---

*England's players were debarred from participating in the IPL by its cricket board.

†South African Haroon Lorgat.

So how long does the window become? Eight weeks? Should they push the English season back by a month? Or end the Australian season early? What about Tests in the West Indies and Sri Lanka? What about the ten-year calendar?

The franchise holders will sit down in the first week of June and see if it has been worth it. Their assessment of success will be based on the number of people who come in through the gates, the number of people who watch and the possibility of merchandising and countering the instantly available fakes in the market. They will also want a few more guarantees with respect to scheduling and, therefore, with the choice of players. Before they sit down for their next round of spending, they will have to know what they are buying. Do they have a player for the entire season? Will he suddenly go away to play a domestic tournament? Franchisees are not in this for mindless spending and they will want a clearer picture next time.

The players will be hoping that it can extend careers or, in some cases, offer choices. Would they want to play county cricket day in, day out for four months in front of fewer spectators than at a dinner table, if they get the same amount of money for playing only six weeks? Will older players find a three-hour game easier to handle or will they be found out by younger players with little respect for age and records? Will the IPL in fact hasten the exit of middle-aged players?

Will cricket remain the staple attraction or will it have to cede way to this curious amalgam of cricket and entertainment (as if either needed a prop!). So far, the only 'entertainment' came from the cheerleaders who cheered with equal enthusiasm, or monotony, for either side. Now, there are movie stars, lead singers, dancers from the United States . . . Is this the way ahead? And what will this do to the traditional, die-hard cricket watcher? My feeling is that the sandwich has got to be full of the real thing but that is something that we will learn as we go along.

And I think the impact will be felt on one-day cricket in a few months as fielding standards improve, definitions of good totals change and exotic deliveries make their appearance. Cricket will not be the same but that does not necessarily mean it will be the worse for it.

WARNE SHOWED THAT CRICKET SPEAKS A UNIVERSAL LANGUAGE

6 June 2008

There are many reasons why the Rajasthan Royals won. Many more will now be unearthed, for every event, significant or otherwise, will now find profound meaning. There are many practitioners of retro-fit, finding weighty answers for normal events when the result is already known. Indeed, Shane Warne will become a better captain with every passing day and he will have a jolly laugh over it—with a beer and a cigarette watching his favourite St Kilda team play footy.

Quite aside from the result, which is more a by-product of great performance than an end in itself anyway, what was wonderful to watch was how a diverse set of people were able to bond under someone they had never met before. The key to it is understanding each player, accepting oddities and insecurities they may have and working with the person as much as with the cricketer.

Many years ago I asked Michael Holding why Clive

Captained by Shane Warne, Rajasthan Royals won the inaugural IPL tournament on 1 June 2008.

23

Lloyd was rated a great captain when really all he had to do was to turn up with the finest set of individuals to take the field together. 'Captaincy isn't so much about tactics as it is about knowing your players and understanding that each is different. We respected Lloydy because he took the trouble to understand us and accepted that we all had our idiosyncrasies,' he said.

The key to team spirit is communication and this would have been Warne's greatest challenge. The only language that his think tank spoke was also the language that a lot of players in the team would have been uncomfortable with. But by gelling so wonderfully, and it was great to see, Warne showed that the language of cricket and the intent to communicate can override strange nouns and verbs. It is a huge learning, one that enemies of foreign coaches would do well to reflect over. Language and culture can be a barrier only for those who choose to look upon it as a barrier.

And yet, having been lucky to have had a ringside view of a lot of the action, if there was one reason I would ascribe to Rajasthan's success, it was that everyone in the team seemed empowered to win. Warne must have made everyone feel special, he certainly did young Ravindra Jadeja.

At the D.Y. Patil Stadium, before play started in the Mumbai Indians vs Rajasthan Royals game, I saw Warne having a quiet puff and so waited till he finished before going over to say hello. In no time, he was by my side, cheerful grin as ever, firm handshake and eager to talk. The Royals were doing well and I told him I was intrigued by his decision to bat Jadeja at no. 6 because we knew him as a left-arm spinner who batted down the order.

'Jadeja? Ah, he's a rockstar mate,' he said and shouted across to the young kid who was about fifty metres away.

'Have you met Harsha?' he said as young Jadeja promptly came skipping across. 'Keep an eye on him mate, he's going to be a star,' he told me even as the young man grinned from ear to ear.

Such pronouncements could work two ways. With the weak, it might lead to the head-in-the-clouds syndrome that has often hurt Indian cricket. With the diligent and ambitious, it could be just the shot of encouragement that a young man craves for. The Royals lost the game that day, there were some strong words spoken in the dressing room but Warne was game for a drink at a party thrown by the opposition that night.

'Just as well it happened now,' he said. 'The team needs to know they can get one of these days and it is best it happens now rather than in a knockout game.'

I also believe Warne's desire to win from any position was infectious. Teams that go in thinking they can lose inevitably do. And one of the reasons Australia have been a force over the years, and Warne is a typical product of the system, is that they always back themselves to win. And you could see that in a line-up that included no more than five batsmen, two of whom, Asnodkar and Pathan, were happy to slog the first ball they faced and a third, Kaif, who was in no form at all. And yet Warne kept playing five batsmen, even playing himself at seven. It was a strategy that could easily have boomeranged but one of the reasons it didn't, I believe, the fact that the players were empowered to be themselves and to search for a win at all times.

I have also heard it said that they were lucky. It's a strange beast, this luck. Why does it seem to knock more often on the door of those that win? Or is it that it knocks on everyone's door and only those that know how to win recognize it?

NOT A BAD PLAN B, BUT THE FANS WILL DEFINITELY BE MISSED

27 March 2009

It is a relief and an accomplishment that the IPL is on. There has been much discussion and debate and that is not wrong because activities on this scale are inevitably going to polarize people. Some of the debate was puerile and fairly devoid of logic, some of it was justified but we live in a democracy, thank God, and there must be room for everyone, including politicians of all hues. If wannabes and society climbers clambered onto the first edition of the IPL, the politicians have sought to own a bit of this time; both types have always been eager to swallow every opportunity that comes their way, anyway.

The IPL won't be the same this year. Having been lucky enough to have had a vantage point last year,* I

The Indian Premier League was moved to South Africa for the second season after several state governments said they would not be able to provide adequate security for the IPL matches since the dates clashed with the general elections in India.

*Harsha Bhogle was part of the Mumbai Indians entourage for the first season of IPL.

26

could see the enthusiasm and the energy that people filled stadiums with. The crowds made IPL 1. Without them it would have been just another tournament; they made it the biggest thing to have happened to cricket. And the players were exceptional in their commitment, most of them at any rate. You had some people of dubious attitude and they stood out but most others immersed themselves into their new teams, sharing knowledge, sparing time for younger players and showing why they had entry into the world of the greats. The players will still be there this year but there will be something missing.

Having said that, we need to weigh what is missing with all that we might have otherwise missed. As the situation grew in complexity, as various actors clambered onto the stage, it was no longer a question of whether or not the IPL should be held in India. It was whether or not the IPL should happen. It was no longer about whether we should have curd rice or pasta but whether we can have dinner at all. And that is what the IPL organizers have done: they have gone in search of a different restaurant because theirs is closed for dinner.

So is Mr Modi* wrong or Mr Chidambaram†? The IPL or the Government of India? Ignore for a moment the language used or the combativeness on display and cut to the options they had. Mr Chidambaram, like a bowler does, used his prerogative to set the field. Now that was given. He wasn't going to provide Central forces (and what a sad moment in itself that the availability of anti-terror forces should be the deciding factor in our game), and he wasn't going to allow state governments to take policemen away from election duty. Now faced with this, the IPL

---

*Lalit Modi, chairman of the Indian Premier League.

†P. Chidambaram, India's home minister.

could either have conceded defeat or played a shot, which is the prerogative of the batsman. They have chosen to play an unconventional shot, a switch-hit if you choose, having used up other options. So now, Mr Chidambaram has what he wants, which is the forces he needs to conduct an election, and Mr Modi has a sub-optimal result, not a boundary maybe but a three, but at least he is batting.

So has the IPL told the world it is unsafe to play sport in India by moving out? No, it hasn't. It has accepted the ground reality that a tournament of this scale in the middle of the world's largest and most complex democratic exercise is unviable. A tournament of this size any other time or a smaller event in the middle of an election is still possible. The Davis Cup tie against Australia, for example, probably doesn't need to be moved out.*

But now everyone needs to look ahead, to make the best of the situation that presents itself. That is what sport teaches you; that there is no point in looking at what might have been, that you try and win the game from the position you are in. And the big plus with moving it overseas is that it allows the brand to acquire a larger global presence. The IPL has created a wow factor across the entire sporting world (yesterday, at a Formula 1 promotional event Shane Warne was asked questions about the IPL) and this is an opportunity to demonstrate it in another land. In another part of the world names like Mumbai Indians, Chennai Super Kings and Delhi Daredevils will enter the minds of sports lovers the way Liverpool, Manchester United and Arsenal have with young Indians. Football leagues have been around much longer and football is many many times the size of cricket but isn't this a

---

*Interestingly, a few days after this piece was written, Australia forfeited the match, refusing to play in India.

delicious thought? That a kid in Cape Town would talk of being a Rajasthan Royals fan or a young man in Durban would want to support the Mumbai Indians?

Moving the IPL to South Africa isn't the best thing that could have happened. But as a fallback option it has much merit.

THE CONCEPT OF TIME-OUTS IN TWENTY20 IS A BIT OUT OF PLACE

8 May 2009

I am delighted that the process of eliminating the time-out (maybe marginalizing is a more appropriate word at the moment) has begun. It was clear that it wasn't working, either for the spectators or the viewers, and that it had to go at some point. And it is nice to see that people are not being dogmatic about it. Two breaks of two and a half minutes each may not hurt the game as much, though that can at best be a stop-gap approach. In the years to come, I won't be surprised if it fades away completely, for it must.

Stripped of its commercial flavour (my friends who watch American sport tell me there are many more commercial intrusions there), it was an attempt to pause, take a backward step and analyse. In theory good, but it goes against the real character of T20 cricket which, at its

---

The second series of IPL introduced a 'strategy break' of seven and a half minutes in the middle of each innings. Most felt it was more of a commercial break. The duration of the break was reduced halfway into the tournament.

heart, is a relentless gladiatorial sport. It is cerebral, as all sport is at various levels from chess to boxing (not WWE because that is not sport!), but its real appeal lies in instinct and the backing of instinct in a short time frame. T20 values people who think on their feet, it rewards initiative as different from the equally enticing Test match format where patience is a virtue, where a storm is allowed to pass and you have time to pick up the debris and rebuild. A time-out in T20 is a bit like allowing a five-over hitting time in a Test match, it's a bit out of place.

A time-out also allows many other theories to enter a captain's mind, many theories from many sources, and I am not sure that is how it should be. For the hour and a half that an innings lasts, the captain must run the ship, take bold and yet calculated decisions, soar or sink with them. He must only have the six balls between an over and the one to follow to decide on the next course of action. It will require the captain to juggle many possibilities in a short period of time, to have his mind working furiously and yet project calm. T20 cricket tests a captain in many different ways than a Test match does—neither is necessarily the superior test for each requires different skills. Is the 5000 metres a more skilful race than the 100 metres? Or does it demand different skills? Even in its infancy, T20 is showing that a good captain is an invaluable asset to possess.

And so as we slip past the halfway point of IPL 2, a frenetic but wonderfully organized event, it is interesting to see who is doing well and who isn't, especially in the light of a call to have more overseas cricketers in the playing eleven.

It is a thought that has been quickly rejected and I believe rightly so. Eventually the IPL, even as it bestows riches on most, must remain an Indian tournament and four overseas players seems just right.

Not surprisingly, indeed almost inevitably, attention has focused on the overseas players, and that is why I looked at the latest MVP rankings on rediff.com with more than usual interest.

Of the top thirty players, irrespective of their price tag, fifteen are Indian. It could be argued that it is no big deal given that fifteen overseas players make the cut out of, for ease of argument, thirty-two that can be used, and that the fifteen Indians who qualify do so from a much larger universe. But remember we are looking at the best among overseas players and so supporters of Indian cricket should be quite happy to see fifteen players there. It is interesting as well that ten of those (Raina, Yusuf Pathan, Irfan Pathan, Yuvraj, R.P. Singh, Pragyan Ojha, Dhoni, Rohit Sharma, Praveen Kumar and Ravindra Jadeja in that order) make the Indian T20 world cup team. The five not in the Indian team are Tendulkar, Kumble, Abhishek Nayar, Dinesh Karthik and Dravid, a big vote for the seniors. Of these Karthik should be disappointed at losing out and Nayar couldn't be far away from making it. But I wonder if it should be a matter of some concern that five players who will almost inevitably make it to the first eleven (Sehwag, Gambhir, Harbhajan, Ishant and Zaheer) seem to be struggling a bit.

That World Cup should be a magnificent spectacle, only maybe a touch short, if anything at all, on the heartwarming moments that a Tyagi, a Suman or a Jakati provide. It is these young players who add the little something to an event.

INDIA HAVE THE FIREPOWER TO GO ALL OUT IN ENGLAND

29 May 2009

So it seems everyone wants to anoint India as favourites for the T20 World Championship. It's a nice thought but it can be a poisoned chalice. In recent times, only Australia have worn the tag of 'favourites' well and as recently as a few days ago the final of the IPL was contested by two teams who weren't on anyone's shortlist!* The longer the game the greater the chance the favourites will come through. If football was played over twenty minutes Manchester United and Barcelona may not have been in the final of the Champions League.

Having said that, India seem to possess the right kind of players: young fellows who get on with it with hardly an eye on the scoreboard. That is the way in this game—one

England would host the second ICC T20 World Championship in June 2009. India were the defending champions.

*On 24 May 2009, the final of IPL 2 was played between Deccan Chargers and Royal Challengers Bangalore, the two lowest ranked teams in the first season of IPL. Deccan Chargers won.

of the most thrilling moments of the IPL was when Sehwag and Dilshan smashed the Deccan Chargers around from a scoreboard that read 0–2. But to be able to do that teams must, ideally, bat deep, and that is where India are well served.

The ideal way to go about it is to have five batsmen, a keeper and a batting all-rounder in the top seven. If there is a second batting all-rounder in that mix, it is even better. no. 8 must necessarily be a bowling all-rounder and of the three bowlers, one should be able to bat. India's top seven are well served on this parameter with Sehwag, Gambhir, Raina, Yuvraj, Rohit Sharma, Dhoni and Yusuf Pathan. Irfan Pathan must be no. 8 and with Harbhajan likely to get in, the batting looks like it has enough to counter most situations.

The bowling can be tricky though. Almost certainly India will play three seamers and Harbhajan (unless Ojha forces his way in, which is not a bad idea) and get the batsmen, at least four of whom bowled well at the IPL, to pitch in as fifth and sixth bowlers. Unfortunately, each of those is a spinner ('slow bowler' might be a more accurate description) and so India will need the conditions to help them just a bit. If, like in South Africa, the ball grips, India will have an embarrassment of riches, but that is unlikely to happen in early-season cricket in England. If it turns out the ball is seaming a fair bit, India might be tempted to play Irfan Pathan at no. 7 and include Praveen Kumar.

Over the last month and a half, teams played with a seven-and-a-half minute break after 10 overs. That can become a habit very quickly and, as we discovered during the IPL, fielding sides who were struggling in the first half were actually waiting for the time-out. And as Anil Kumble told me, he always put his best bowler on during the eleventh over. Now teams will play 20 overs without a break, indeed that is how it had always been till IPL 2, and that will mean even greater emphasis on the captain to be able to think on his feet.

With the exception of Sehwag and Gambhir, by their own standards, each of the Indian players has done well at the IPL and are in form. Sometimes we can raise too many questions about fatigue and ignore the fact that a player in form wants to play more games. If I were Suresh Raina or Rohit Sharma I would be waiting for 6 June, when India plays its first match—even the 1st and the 3rd, in fact, when the teams play warm-up games.

I would also be very keen to see how England host the World T20—the last time they hosted a big event, the 1999 World Cup, they were efficient, as they always are, but there was no atmosphere. There was a job given to them and they carried it out as well as they normally do. But will we have the bugles, the DJs, the noise, or will it be sterile? England is the one country that, in spite of pioneering T20 cricket, has never come to terms with the success of the IPL. I will be disappointed if the tickets are expensive (they should never be once TV rights guarantees you revenue), if bugles are banned and there is no celebration in the stands. This is a new game and we need to look at it differently.

GOOD TEAMS DON'T BECOME BAD OVERNIGHT

19 June 2009

It wasn't that long ago, twenty-seven months isn't that long, that we indulged in a familiar orgy of breast beating after crashing out of a World Cup. Now that situation is upon us again and doubtlessly it will return in our lifetime. Sport is like that; reputations count for only a little and the better side on the day wins. West Indies and England were better than India at Lord's, and anybody would have been better at Nottingham.

So were India a good team that played below par or were they overrated? It is easy to assume the latter, but good teams don't become bad overnight. They might pick up bad habits, a disease somewhere, they might occasionally need a kick up the backside, some deficiencies might surface, but they do not become bad teams. As recently as in the warm-up game (a colossal misnomer!) against Pakistan two weeks ago, India looked in sizzling form.

Defending world T20 champions India crashed out of the second World T20 Championship in the Super 8 stage. Pakistan went on to win the tournament.

It is interesting to look back at that game. Rohit Sharma seemed to belong at the top of the order, his shots took your breath away at times and it seemed that Sehwag may not be missed after all. Sharma's batting was one of the highlights of that game, but the turning point came early in the Pakistan innings when they were finding every boundary on the ground. Suresh Raina hit the stumps directly and Pakistan never really recovered from there.

It happens all the time. Big wins are fashioned by little things done well and it was the little things India did in South Africa that helped win the title two years ago. Against the West Indies at Lord's, it was the catches by Simmons and Fletcher that stopped India, and against England, Stuart Broad timed his jump perfectly to ensure that Jadeja's shot didn't sail over him for six.

By contrast, India were slow in the field. Suresh Raina and Rohit Sharma look good, not world beaters but good, and there are at least four slow movers in the deep. But the most worrisome is Yuvraj Singh. Not long ago, he was electric at point, hit the stumps from anywhere and was among the best fielders in the world. I don't know if it is the knee injury that is hampering him but he is now a shadow of the fielder he was even as his frame grows larger.

But in the end, as Dhoni pointed out, it was the batting that let India down. Anil Kumble, who was with us in the studio, believes 75 per cent of matches are won by the batsmen and indeed, batting has always been India's strong suit. It was one area that nobody believed India would have trouble in, especially after the IPL and after a couple of encouraging performances from Gambhir after that. But here, he wasn't the dominant batsman he can be and Dhoni has now evolved from a punisher into a nudger. Maybe it was by design initially, but it is now part of him, though I sense, based on what he said after India's exit, that he will renew his search for the destroyer who still lurks within him.

The other major difference with the IPL that was overlooked by all of us, and which became increasingly apparent, was that at the World T20, teams have four or five quality bowlers. By contrast, the Deccan Chargers played the second half of the event with no more than two good bowlers in R.P. Singh and Pragyan Ojha. The Royal Challengers had to slip in five or six overs somewhere and even the Chennai Super Kings had a couple of bowlers who were in no danger of playing for India. There is, therefore, always a bowler or two who can be targeted. At the World T20 the runs had to come off quality bowlers except maybe, in the game against the West Indies. Maybe batting is easier in the IPL.

There is much talk of injuries, but that is an essential part of playing at this level. The greats have always overcome injury to play for the country in a major event so the odd player carrying an injury is not unusual. But fatigue is. And that is something each player knows and cannot hide. Being on tour for long periods is part of the job now, and players must rest and train to counter that. It is a personal responsibility and one that is non-negotiable. South Africa have been one of the best teams in this tournament, and one of the sharpest in the field, and they went into the IPL after draining back-to-back Test and one-day series against Australia. Most of their players were at the IPL too. If India's players are fatigued they need to look within.

India still have a good captain and still have a good team. One tournament loss doesn't change that.

THERE IS NOW LIFE BEYOND INTERNATIONALS

16 October 2009

I must confess I am enjoying being a little part of a quiet new revolution in world cricket, of being in this wonderful and disarming global village. The Airtel Champions League is an idea that is finding its feet and, if you measure its success by the quality of cricket and the opportunity it is giving players who were otherwise confined to narrower worlds, it has already worked. Admittedly there are other tools to measure success and the more crucial ones are whether enough people are coming to the ground or watching at home. You can be sure those issues will be addressed because there are large investments at stake, but purely from a cricketing point of view, I am excited.

There is now life beyond international cricket as we knew it and for that alone we must rejoice. There are few things that stir people's emotions more than nation versus

---

The inaugural Champions League T20, a competition between club teams from India, Australia, South Africa, England, West Indies, Sri Lanka and New Zealand, was held in October 2009 in Hyderabad.

nation contests, and that will never change, but that is a smaller, more exalted world. Sport, indeed any pursuit in life, must allow as many people as possible to display their ability, to parade their skills and a nation versus nation contest can be restrictive.

It could never, for example, allow you to experience the combination of disbelief and joy that we saw with Alfonso Thomas of Somerset. Not many people knew much about him, we knew that he was a cricketer, no more, but against the Deccan Chargers he kept his cool, took his side home and then produced one of the most wonderfully innocent and unrestrained exhibitions of happiness I have seen. 'I can't believe what I've done' he gushed and for that moment alone I thought the Champions League was worth it. There are two ways of globalizing a game. One is to allow as many countries as possible to play it and the ICC is, very quietly, doing a very nice job. The other is to allow as many players as possible a stage on which to perform. This is what I hope the Champions League, and in course of time all the feeder tournaments, will do.

Somerset didn't have as good a game when they played Trinidad and Tobago but I enjoyed that game just as much. Trinidad were better than the West Indies team I have seen in recent times and it showed us that Samuel Badree and Sherwin Ganga, to name just two, can play good cricket. Out of the anonymity, and the mess, that is West Indies cricket, here is a team that can play together and dream of a big prize. Our game will grow and will embrace many more on this world stage, and that can only be good for its health.

I see only a couple of problem areas ahead. The first is the bond that must be created between a player and his audience. And for that to happen a player cannot, quite literally, wear different caps. I was on air when Ross Taylor came out to bat for the Royal Challengers Bangalore against the Otago Volts and, in spite of having seen a bit of cricket recently, I was taken aback by the spontaneity, and indeed the intensity, of the welcome he received. Now should his team in New Zealand qualify for the Champions League next year, he cannot walk out at the Chinnaswamy Stadium in different colours. I know this is early days but that would be cheating the fans and their affection. The Champions League and the IPL will grow on the deep connect that exists between fan and sportsman. We need to nurture and respect that connect because the league does not exist without the fan.

The other concern is that far too much depends on the health of one nation's economy and the investment it is willing to make in one sport. If India grows tired of cricket, or if the fans feel let down, the entire structure will collapse. And that is why it is critical, in these good times for franchise-based cricket, to invest in building loyalty. In the next three to five years, franchises should have started becoming global brands. Then everybody will get the confidence to invest more in franchises around the world, which in turn will lead to greater opportunity for players and more fun for fans.

But this is a good beginning. Now we only need to get more people in for non-home games. But that is for another day!

IT'S WORRYING THAT FEW INDIAN CRICKETERS WANT TO BE ATHLETES

17 September 2010

India's cricketers have always looked at fielding the way a chef might a chutney in a thali: it's there to complete the offering, occasionally add some zing to the meal, but you wouldn't practise making it the way you would the main course. Cricket was always about batting and bowling, mainly batting, and fielding was what you did to warm up or something you had to do at the end of training, just before the shower. It wasn't something that defined you, and so good fielders have always been talked about like the distant aunt remembered only for her pickle.

But as the game becomes shorter, as the menu shrinks and every bite becomes important, fielding, cricket's country cousin, is demanding to be heard. When you have just a hot dog the mustard becomes important or, since I'm vegetarian, when you eat only a dosa the chutney is critical. And so, India's cricketers, brought up on batting

---

This piece was written during the second Champions League T20, which was held in South Africa in September 2010, and which Chennai Super Kings won.

and bowling, are looking out of place, like they don't belong. Singles hit to them are becoming twos, catches are falling short and direct hits are infrequent. With only 120 balls to play, the one percenters are getting more and more important and young India is looking the other way.

You saw that when the Mumbai Indians played with teflon hands against the Highveld Lions and the Southern Redbacks. And you saw the importance of it when Davey Jacobs and the Warriors from Port Elizabeth fielded like every ball was their last in the game. Jacobs himself created two wickets with his fielding and those really turned the game their way against the Bushrangers from Victoria. In the 20-overs game fielding is nudging its way up the value chain; a fielder who saves 15 and scores 20 is better than a batsman who scores 40 and lets 10 go!

At Durban you saw the difference in athleticism between the Mumbai Indians and the Southern Redbacks. Daniel Harris created a catch when Ambati Rayudu was well set and saw two go down when it was his turn to bat. So what is it about India? Why is it that we rarely produce athletes? At different times in history India have been a very good catching side but rarely an athletic one and that is increasingly what T20 demands. Is it a gene? Is it the hard outfields that make diving a hazard? I'm not convinced of either answer.

The importance of diving in fielding is grossly overemphasized. The best fielders don't always need to dive since they get to the ball quicker. And that means the time required to accelerate must be small. It can only come with practice but, while a coach can teach you that, a player must feel it from within. It is the same as studying mathematics, preparing for the ballet or cooking a fine dish. If you feel the need to, you will do what it takes. And it worries me that not enough Indian players want to be athletes even though it gives them a better chance of being selected, as with Satheesh of Tamil Nadu and the Mumbai Indians, though he too, I suspect, shines brighter because of the lethargy that defines his surroundings.

So too with the throwing arm. Five throws rifled in from the deep can save five runs and, once you build a reputation for a great throwing arm, you save even more. Increasingly too, as the boundaries come in, you no longer need to throw seventy yards, but even over sixty yards a fielder must feel the need to practise, to save his side that extra run and in doing so, add one to his contribution to the side.

India's ambition to remain a world power on the cricket field, as opposed to off it, will depend on how quickly the new generation adapts to the requirements of the shortest form and on whether they have the rigour to sustain their game in Test cricket. The requirements are vastly different and the shortcomings stand out increasingly. India is still the top Test side, a legacy of the cricket a departing generation played, but are struggling in T20 cricket, the trademark of the new kids on the block! Maybe there is a story there.

ODIs

DON'T THROW THE RULE BOOK, GIVE IT A CHANCE

15 July 2005

To a scientist, there is a romance associated with the laboratory, a cradle where some of the most invaluable discoveries are conceived and nurtured, where spectacular failures haunt every corner. But the two go together on the path towards evolution. Failure is the pit stop on the road to success; wrong is a step up the ladder of right. It isn't quite so with the philosopher, not for him the mandatory observation before the inference.

Cricket sadly has been in the midst of philosophers, rather than scientists. The moment change is announced, it gets denounced; an oracle pops up at every street corner to pronounce doom, observation becomes irrelevant and the cricket ground as a laboratory suffers harm. It was the ancestors of this breed of critics who castigated Galileo when he suggested that the Earth may not be the centre of the universe!

This piece was written soon after the ICC introduced the supersub as an experiment, and increased the number of overs with fielding restrictions from 15 to 20 (now known as power plays).

And so it is with the two recent innovations to one-day cricket. They look good, on the scanty evidence of three one-day matches; in certain conditions they seem to have the odd limitation but they need to be given a chance. A chance to succeed and indeed a chance to fail.

We need to see whether they work. If they don't, we can go back to the original method of playing; but knowing that they don't work is a learning too. Knowing that carbon dioxide doesn't support burning was a valuable conclusion.

Already we have some interesting knowledge and that can only evolve as one-day cricket is played in different conditions. We can already tell that the power play initiative will prove more decisive on the subcontinent or on flat batting pitches.

In our part of the world captains waited, often desperately, for the 15-over mark to spread out the field. Now they can do so after 10 but slotting in the remaining 10 overs will be very tricky. In relatively easier bowling conditions, like in England or, I suspect, in New Zealand, fielding captains can use all 20 overs at once.

What is true as well is that the power plays reward teams with wicket-taking bowlers. On the acceptable assumption that a fielding captain wants to get rid of the 20 overs as soon as possible, a wicket-taking bowler setting the batting side back will be invaluable.

The more the wickets gained, the quicker the overs consumed; to that extent, the power play innovation actually rewards aggressive bowlers—which is what cricket was meant to do. Brett Lee did that consistently and set it up for Australia in the last two games against England.

It is clear, though, that the power plays will eventually lead to more runs and that means good fielding and catching will, if anything, become even more critical. You will notice, as this argument builds up, that the two innovations actually reward better teams. That is particularly true of the supersub and it is interesting that neither captain in the three games we have seen seems particularly enamoured of it.

I say 'interesting' because it helps Australia and, against any team other than Australia, would help England as well. Indeed, it will help any team that has a complete eleven and can do without the twelfth. Teams that bank on the supersub to lend completeness to their offering will be the ones in most trouble.

It has been suggested that the supersub rule helps teams that bat second. That need not necessarily be true but what it definitely does is to reward teams that win the toss and that is a limitation.

If, for example, a team has picked five batsmen, a keeper and five bowlers with a batsman as a sub, they can win the toss, bowl first and then sub a bowler for a batsman. If however they lose the toss and have to bat first, they have to decide whether to go ahead with only five batsmen or sub early and give up a bowler for the additional batsman.

In that case they need at least two of their batsmen to bowl and so teams that do not have that flexibility, that do not have enough all-rounders, will suffer.

Indeed, the supersub rule makes all-rounders invaluable and that will help England, Pakistan and South Africa and, with the strong presence of Andrew Symonds, give Australia some help too. India and the West Indies would seem likely to be the worst hit, Sri Lanka would struggle in seaming conditions and New Zealand on tracks that need spinners.

More and more the game will move towards multi-skilled players and that cannot be bad.

The interesting variation would have been to announce

the twelfth man after the toss. The team that batted first would play seven batsmen and sub one in the break, the team that bowled first would play five bowlers and sub a bowler for a batsman later.

It would allow batsmen to be up against good bowlers all the time, marginally reduce the importance of the all-rounder and allow specialists to be picked and, to that extent, equalize all teams.

Time may point out more flaws or might conclude this to be a master stroke. But we need to give it time, to observe and then to draw conclusions.

Otherwise, like the church in Galileo's time, we will stifle innovation and fresh thought. And remember, the church was proved wrong then!

A 'YAHOO' MOMENT FROM SACHIN'S BACK PAGES

27 October 2005

Long before he overcame Sri Lanka's bowlers at Nagpur, Sachin Tendulkar won the battle against his deadliest opponent. Besieged by injury, Tendulkar had allowed himself to believe that there were now things he could not do, that being the senior statesman meant he had to impose limitations on himself.

His powers of auto-suggestion, like his other powers, were substantial. Tendulkar became polite to bowlers, sometimes made them look better than they were, he nudged the ball and placed it gently. It was like the Bachchan of *Deewar* playing the Bachchan of *Alaap*. He was very good at it, but it wasn't him.

The trance had to break some day, he had to cast aside his suit and put on his sneakers again. He had to rediscover himself, look into the mirror and realize that the man looking back at him was thirty-two, not forty-five. I suspect it happened two days before the match at Nagpur.

In the ODI against Sri Lanka at Nagpur on 25 October 2005, Tendulkar, coming back from injury, scored a match-winning 93.

It was a liberated Tendulkar that walked out to bat, one who had overcome the burdens he had imposed on himself. This was the child again, the same joyous little boy with his toys; he skipped from one dinky car to the other, pulled out the remote-controlled bike and cheerfully sprayed the world with his water pistol. He played the straight drive again, lofted the fast bowler, teasingly lapped the ball to fine leg and unleashed the cover-drive.

It happens to the best. The mind is made up and instinct is buried. We seek to become conformists, from making the rules we bow to them. Sometimes we grow weary with battle, the next conquest becomes daunting. We start looking at obstacles rather than opportunities, worry about getting out rather than think of scoring runs; once again we see the fielders not the gaps between them.

And we need to be convinced about our own skills. We own them but we don't trust them anymore and that is when the environment becomes critical. Stars who are surrounded by people who tell them they can do no wrong start stagnating because fresh thought doesn't reach them anymore, the contrary view becomes outlawed, even unpardonable.

Somebody broke Tendulkar's defensive mindset. Maybe he did it himself, maybe he listened and agreed but the end result was that he drove past his own barriers. The journey was thrilling, it was almost as if the result didn't matter. And so he played the shots he wouldn't, and some he couldn't because of his left elbow.

Now the Sri Lankans will be worried. He may still get out early, he may still miscue shots, that cheeky run might be nipped by the direct hit but he now seeks to dominate, which is what he was born to do. He sees himself as the striker again, not the mid-fielder who feeds the ball; Shammi Kapoor is saying 'Yahoo' again, not reciting Ghalib.

As captain, Rahul Dravid couldn't ask for more. Indeed he made a handsome contribution himself, batting positively and taking the big decision. But it was typical of the man that on one of his best days, he chose to look at the wider picture; to remind people that on another day not everything might come off, that Pathan is still a bowler who bats! All captains look good when Tendulkar is firing.

Indeed the magnificent Jayasuriya might play the kind of innings that Tendulkar did, Sangakkara might show off his skills and the wicketkeeper's lapses might prove to be costly. Catches might fall a foot farther away and run-outs might be missed.

But India have made a beginning and it is a bold one. They will stumble but if they want to rise from number seven, this is the only way.

ON CRICKET'S SENSEX, INDIA ARE A PROMISING MID-CAP STOCK

17 February 2006

Through good deed or fortune India have one outstanding captain following another; each well suited for the situation confronting Indian cricket. Many players have stood out for India in this one-day triumph but no one more than Rahul Dravid. He has combined steel with aggression and he has been his own man. Those who feared that Dravid's innate goodness might make him soft have been proved wrong.

Sourav Ganguly worked very well with youngsters. He did so in a flamboyant, big-brotherly style and made uncertain minds feel at home on the big stage. He wasn't a method person but he rallied troops outstandingly and they followed him.

Dravid is a lot more understated, his aggression is less visible, more perceived. He inspires respect with deeds, willing to take the tough job and, in doing so, stating his case. Barry Richards once said of Ian Chappell, 'He would

---

In February 2006, India won the five-match ODI series in Pakistan 4–1 under Rahul Dravid's stewardship.

never ask anyone to do something he wouldn't do himself', and Dravid comes from that school.

I suspect Dravid's troops march alongside him. It's more '*saathi haath badhaana saathi re*' rather than '*chalo veer jawaano*'. Each has its merits.

A good side finds the man for the moment; each believing that he can win a game rather than watch someone else do it, as happens in individual-dominated teams. Indeed that is the strength of this side and I think a vision is slowly taking shape. Dhoni one day, Yuvraj on another, and now Suresh Raina of whom much more lies undiscovered.

Each is seizing the opportunity that presents itself and that can only come from self-belief. India might still have some distance to cover in Test cricket but the projections in one-day cricket are looking good. It is a very promising mid-cap stock at the moment.

The key to a good one-day side lies in the combination of players; not great solo artists but ensemble musicians each capable of playing a great note but also of contributing to the overall score. Australia can do that consistently, England under certain conditions and Pakistan devastatingly so when the air is right. India are getting there too for against a good side they are able to play eight batsmen and four bowlers.

India are also discovering the great strengths of flexibility. If anyone can play anywhere then players aren't missed as much when they have to sit out. So Pathan can bat at no. 3 or 8, Dhoni at 4 or 7 and Dravid anywhere. It also means that on some days India can play seven batsmen and five bowlers, which is a combination that most teams dream of.

To achieve that a team needs three all-rounders: a wicketkeeper who can bat, a 10-overs man who can bat in the top seven and a batsman in the top five capable of giving 5 overs a game consistently.

India are a bit thin in category three at the moment and that is where Sachin Tendulkar has played such a key role in the last two games. By bowling 19 overs in two games for 2 wickets and at just over 4 an over, Tendulkar has allowed India to play Raina. A floater is a privilege few teams are allowed but Tendulkar cannot do this all the time. And that is why the key to India taking the next step ahead lies with Virender Sehwag, the bowler.

If Sehwag can take his bowling one step up—it has fallen two paces behind in the last year—India could field four seamers if the situation demands. And if they are confronted with a dry surface, he can give Harbhajan much-needed support. Then with Tendulkar capable of bowling either slow spin or seam up, India will have a bowling attack for any surface.

Indeed four seamers seems to be the way to go on most days and India can either do so with Harbhajan playing for Raina or indeed not playing at all; a lateral thought many might not have considered six months ago.

But every thought needs suitable action. And that means a team must possess players with the skills to carry out plans. All along India could never play five bowlers even if that was the most obvious plan because it left the batting too thin, not to speak of a makeshift keeper. Now, on most days, India can. If they believe four bowlers will do, it gives them great strength down the order with the bat. It doesn't mean India will win every game they play, but they give themselves the best possible chance of doing so.

But the main reason India are looking smart is that they are fielding smart. Kaif, Yuvraj and Raina are electric, Dravid has excellent hands, Pathan and Agarkar have strong arms and quick legs and Dhoni is getting better. India, once again, have the grammar right.

Dravid and Chappell* have the right men in the right places. Now they need to find consistency if they seek to set up base camp two on the way to Everest.

---

*Greg Chappell, India's coach at the time.

HE'S BACK, AND HOW

15 September 2006

Of all the cricketers I have met, or seen, over the years, nobody resembles the child more than Sachin Tendulkar does. Three hundred and sixty-four games old, he still approaches every match with the excitement with which a kid might navigate an old dinky car round the dining table. Indeed the game and its implements are his toys and without them he is lost, listless. His mind wanders, like Calvin's might, only in this case he is Spaceman Spiff himself.

Take away his toys and there is no Tendulkar.

And so while we were looking forward to this game, it would bear no relation to the restlessness within him. He wanted to play this game far more than we wanted him to. This excitement, eighteen years into his profession, separates him from those that, on some days, look upon playing cricket as a job.

You have to admit he managed his comeback just

On 14 September 2006, Tendulkar returned from injury to score an unbeaten 141 against the West Indies at Kuala Lumpur. This was his fortieth ODI century.

right. There were many, including me, who thought he would be best served playing some county cricket in England where decent bowlers would try their best to get him out. He chose instead to go on a little picnic playing cricket at Lashings. He knew his shoulder wasn't good enough yet, he knew that if he was playing a serious, competitive cricket match, he would get into the mood of it and let fly a ripper of seventy-five yards. He wanted to play himself at a more relaxed pace.

Some of you might remember a little line from Tatenda Taibu that was tucked away in the midst of those easy runs he was scoring for Lashings. 'His shoulder didn't seem right,' Taibu said. Tendulkar knew what he was doing.

It reminded me of a story Navjot Sidhu often tells about Sunil Gavaskar. In the build-up to the Reliance Cup of 1987, Gavaskar, then thirty-seven, wasn't too keen to bat in the nets. He'd knock a few balls every day and that was it. Sidhu says that on the big day, his first scoring shot was a delectable straight drive off Bruce Reid. Great players know their body and their mind better than most, they know when to rise to the challenge for truth be told, they sometimes get bored if there isn't one!

In some ways, this was a programmed hundred from Tendulkar. The hypothesis has always been that if Tendulkar bats 40 overs, he will get a century. And in pretty good time. Forty overs is normally about 250 balls and since Tendulkar rotates the strike better than most, he normally ends up getting no more than 110–120 balls out of 250. And that means a century from about 120 balls or fewer with the promise of more in the last few overs.

In this game, he got his century from 119 balls on a rather moody pitch and, with great poise, ensured that he was there at the end. Interestingly, that is something he hasn't always done. If there was one thing we did not know enough about Tendulkar in one-day cricket, it was his batting in the slog overs.

By batting through, he has now climbed another peak, only a little one compared to the many mountains he scales regularly but one that will satisfy him and drive him in the last stage of his career. It might seem a small goal for one so imposing, but as people grow bigger and more successful their goals diminish. I won't be surprised at all if batting beyond the 40th and as close to the 50th becomes a motivator for Tendulkar in the games ahead.

It is a goal that the team will endorse heartily. But as we celebrate, we need to tuck away at the back of our minds the fact that this will not happen every day. Tendulkar is in a reality show, not a scripted blockbuster, and he will slip. This is not Amitabh Bachchan with Salim–Javed, or to be more relevant to a newer audience, this is not *Jhalak Dikhla Ja*.

Let us not package him like the movies, just savour him for what he has done and is doing for as long as he can.

I'M NOT SURE IF PLAYING FOUR BOWLERS IS THE WAY TO GO

23 March 2007

There is too much anger in the air. Anger. Hostility. Abuse. In public, on blogs, in social gatherings. And it is either derived from or aimed at the game that we profess to love. We claim to be admirers but we are fickle and those that are fickle are not really friends. We rave and we rant and we beat our breasts and we throw stones and pull walls down and believe that is acceptable. And then a day later, we go overboard; we queue up to sign meaningless messages, we tell our young cricketers that they are superheroes and we create comic strips. But it's only a cricket match and the other team wants to win it as well. And has a right to.

But we fail to use the one weapon that we possess that is deadlier than any other. It is the off button on the remote control. But we can't do that, we cannot treat

---

India began the 2007 ICC World Cup disastrously by losing its group match to Bangladesh. This meant that they had to win their last group match against Sri Lanka on 23 March 2007 or be eliminated in the first round of a tournament they were fancied to win. India lost the match, and crashed out of the tournament.

triumph and disaster as impostors. We need our daily fix. Cricket is our punching bag and our calming pillow. And our cricketers are the bewildered recipients of both. We accept conspiracy theories without evidence and we bestow supernatural powers on young men.

I think it is time to see what the younger generation thinks; a generation that we have let down with our irrationality. They are saying 'Just cool it, man' and I cannot think of four better words. So, maybe, we should all 'just cool it', sit down and watch India vs Sri Lanka if we want to, and should India lose, be large-hearted to say well played to our soft-spoken, less-hyped and polite neighbours. And accept the fact that if opponents win they do so because they played better, not because we played badly. The idea that we are the centre of the universe was found to be flawed many hundreds of years ago!

And let's face it, Sri Lanka are looking the better side at the moment and one major reason is that they bowl better. And because we are a suspect bowling side, their batting is likely to look better too. But more than anything else, I think Sri Lanka will start favourites because they look more relaxed, less anxious. The team that is too tense and too pumped up will make it difficult for itself.

I must confess I am a little worried about India's bowling. Zaheer Khan and Munaf Patel are bowling quite well but Ajit Agarkar has looked fragile. He is at his best when he swings the ball back into the left-handers early on and at the moment, he is merely hitting the deck behind a good length. And Anil Kumble, big-hearted and clever, just seems to have lost the 'rocket' ball, the one that fizzes out of the pitch at an uncomfortable pace. It is a bowling side that needs support, and that is why I am not sure if playing four bowlers is the way to go. Yes, Sehwag and Tendulkar exist and they are fine as back-up bowlers but should one of the lead bowlers have a bad day and they have to bowl more than three or four overs, the team is in trouble.

However, if India persist with playing seven batsmen, they are better off chasing a target rather than setting one. Ideally, if a team is worried and anxious it is better to get the runs on the board first, but given the bowling weaknesses it might be better for the stronger arm to take the pressure of winning a match.

It was interesting that when Sri Lanka played Bangladesh the pitch did not do as much as it did during the India–Bangladesh game. These 9.30 a.m. starts are giving the bowling side a half-hour head start, especially if is a bit cloudy in the morning. But on Wednesday the track looked a lot more settled and if that is the case on Friday morning as well, it might take away some of the advantage of winning the toss.

I will also be interested to see if India bat freely even if they lose a couple of wickets early on. One of the reasons teams play seven batsmen is to guard against this, but the moment India lose wickets they tend to stiffen up. And since twos are becoming ones and threes are becoming twos with alarming regularity, the scoreboard tends to stiffen up as well.

It is a game that India must win, but then, if you want to win the World Cup, you have to win crunch games. This one has just come a little early, that's all.

SENIORS ARE THE BLUE-CHIP STOCKS, SURE TO DELIVER

Sachin Tendulkar is right, 400 is just a number. It is also a monument, not yet a memorial! It is a monument to longevity as much as it is to excellence, passion and fitness. It is not just an acknowledgement of the fact that you are good enough to be picked 400 times but of the fact that you don't mind young men running in trying to knock your head off, stump you short, sneak another run from you in the deep and snarl at you the way you wouldn't allow your son to!

It is also an aspirational number for an older man who has befriended youth and managed to get so far. When you look at players good enough to play three or four hundred games you don't analyse them every match, or every four matches. These are blue chip stocks that might see dips but which inevitably deliver over a wider horizon. You sell them for meteoric stocks at your peril.

Sachin Tendulkar played his 400th one-day international at Vadodara against Australia on 11 October 2007. When asked about his achievement, he said, 'Four hundred is just a number.'

So is it time for these blue chips to be phased out? If India's success at Twenty20 is the argument, it is a flawed one because a quick 25 doesn't quite have the same ring to it over 50 overs. And yet, fearless youth need to be given an opportunity. The idea of rotating the seniors seems sound when spoken but tends to weaken before the primary objective of putting the best possible side on the park every time. Is Rohit Sharma a better player than Rahul Dravid in current form? Is Robin Uthappa a stronger alternative to Sourav Ganguly?

Sometimes, faced as we are by dizzying changes, we tend to believe that is the solution. It is merely an alternative path and one that we must assess with care. The end of this series against Australia might be a good time to pause and reflect on the path that the selectors need to choose. The last two games will be very interesting. But it isn't only the seniors there is a buzz about. This series has been played with extraordinary rancour and some strangely holier-than-thou statements have surfaced. The best sound in this game is still that of one object on another; willow upon leather; bat upon stump or pad, ball hitting palm. The moment the lip starts dominating, the game loses something and there is no doubt this series has been the poorer for the dialogues, largely inane, on the field and in print.

You can see why India came out firing and into Aussie domain. It is not always that those that give can take in equal measure and, by turning the heat on Australia, India wanted to see if the pressure got to the visitors. It did, but sadly India's verbal aggression wasn't mirrored on the field and maybe India need to do it differently, be a little more selective, a little shrewder. And there is no greater aggression that an outswinger beautifully bowled, or a pull shot jauntily played or a catch easily taken or the stumps scattered from an acute angle. The high ground in a high-stakes game belongs to he who is calm in the mind.

It doesn't always matter what gestures the body makes or what sounds escape the lips as long as the mind is calm, ready and poised. And that is something that Sreesanth must learn. He can either resemble a clown, which he does sometimes, or he can seek to play the monk, which will be disastrous. He needs to find the middle ground, some place to channel his inherent aggression. He cannot lose it but his aggression cannot lead him astray. A few evenings with Anil Kumble, the most aggressive Indian bowler I have seen, will not be wasted.

INDIA IS FINALLY GETTING A
ONE-DAY POOL

13 June 2008

The fortune-teller and the forecaster, each indignant at
being clubbed with the other, rarely get it right in India.
The world, for example, hasn't ended yet, though some
might believe we've tried hard enough. And the dollar, like
an errant child, always goes the other way. And yet here I
am taking a call on the future of Indian cricket. Truly, as
modern bards have said, we are like that only!

For long, some of us have been hoping that India
creates a pool of twenty to twenty-five players from which
the national team can be chosen, from which any selection
of eleven could play to approximately the same level. I
know it doesn't always work that way, Ronaldo would
weaken any team by his absence, but good teams hope to
get there. I believe that in one-day cricket, India are well
on course. The team that beat Pakistan so easily in Dhaka
was without Tendulkar, Harbhajan, Sreesanth, Zaheer

This piece was written during the tri-series in Bangladesh in June
2008.

Khan and R.P. Singh, five names who would make a first eleven on most days.

So here is the list that excites me greatly: Sachin Tendulkar, Virender Sehwag, Gautam Gambhir, Yuvraj Singh, Rohit Sharma, Suresh Raina, Robin Uthappa, S. Badrinath, Yusuf Pathan, Piyush Chawla, Harbhajan Singh, Amit Mishra, Irfan Pathan, Ishant Sharma, R.P. Singh, Sreesanth, Praveen Kumar, Zaheer Khan, M.S. Dhoni, Dinesh Karthik and Parthiv Patel. To this list, add Test cricket stalwarts Anil Kumble, Rahul Dravid, V.V.S. Laxman and Sourav Ganguly and you have as fine a batch of twenty-five players as any country could hope for.

The first thing that strikes you is how young the one-day side is. Even if you take some of the ages with the necessary pinch of salt, it is still a collection that one can look ahead with. Of those that played that game against Pakistan, only Sehwag had made his debut in the decade of the nineties, a mere two years after Harbhajan Singh had first appeared, but a full decade after Tendulkar, who must necessarily be looked at differently while discussing longevity.

Happily, there is competition for every spot and that means players will have to be on their toes; a quality that Indian cricket has not always been blessed with. Piyush Chawla is making the most of Harbhajan's absence and Sehwag and Gambhir could raise questions on how much Tendulkar will be missed. At the moment though, this is an excellent fair-weather batting side and on tracks responsive to quality seam and swing bowling, the top order still needs to prove it can do without Tendulkar.

And they can field. Except for R.P. Singh, Praveen Kumar and Zaheer Khan, you really don't need to hide anyone and for the first time, you get the feeling that maybe young Indian players are getting contemporary. It's a great time though to raise the bar and make this an intimidating fielding side. The bar doesn't have to be raised by too much, but as high jumpers and pole vaulters will tell you it is the last few centimetres that actually make the difference. The key will be attitude and that is the one variable we can look at with great curiosity. Too many players in this side have had slumps that could be attributed to attitude. This is where Gary Kirsten's* real test will come. These boys can play but can they now stretch ambition and show they have what it takes to reach there.

I wish the BCCI takes this aspect a bit more seriously. With Harbhajan, Sreesanth and Praveen Kumar, in recent times, they have players who have struggled to cope with the position they find themselves in. And they are by no means the only three. It may not earn anyone any money but it is no less crucial to the strength of Indian cricket that young men learn to cope. To possess aggression but to find the moment to release it is a great, and therefore, elusive quality.

I like one other aspect of this side. There is far greater flexibility, there are people who can play in different positions and I believe the Pathan brothers are representative of this. Yusuf can bat anywhere and bowl off spin; Irfan is ideal in the lower middle order and, if he can't lay his hands on the new ball, in the middle and end overs. Now if Yusuf Pathan can bowl a bit more and Chawla can bat a bit more, the side will have the perfect balance to it, except for just one slot. A top-order batsman who can bowl seam-up. Till that man is sighted, this team will remain far more formidable in Indian conditions than in conditions that favour quicker bowling.

---

*India's new coach.

I will be very disappointed, given that World Cup 2011 is on the subcontinent, if this squad of cricketers doesn't make India favourites to win it, recent performances of forecasters and fortune-tellers notwithstanding.

THERE HAS NEVER BEEN A MOMENT LIKE THE '83 WORLD CUP WIN

23 June 2008

Is it already twenty-five years then? Should the memories be acquiring a little sepia edge to them? Then why do I remember every moment of that game? To a generation that thinks yesterday was a million miles away, twenty-five years must seem like the Mughals and the East India company all over again. But they must know the enormity, however improbable it was at that moment, of what happened on the 25th of June 1983.

There was no huge build-up. There couldn't be. Six previous World Cup games had produced one win, against lowly East Africa, and India were finding their feet in limited-overs cricket. Only forty one-dayers had been played over eleven years and twenty-eight of them had been lost. The World Cup meant a week in England in mid-June. This time it might be a bit longer since each team played each other twice. In spite of that, the World Cup was a mere sixteen-day affair. Had it not been for World Series

---

On 25 June 2008, India celebrated the silver jubilee of its one and only World Cup win.

Cricket, and the events in Australia, it might have remained as short as most modern weddings.

There were some signs, though, that things might be changing. A couple of wins had materialized in Australia (wins were as difficult to find then as a melody in a Himesh Reshamiyya album or a hit from the Ramgopal Varma factory), and much to everyone's astonishment the mighty West Indies had been beaten at home for the first time.

And, as I read through an amateur analysis I had made for the *Deccan Chronicle* on 4 June 1983, I discover that Kim Hughes had labelled India the dark horses. The fan in me had tried to make out a case for India to qualify for the semi-final and, the day after the article had appeared, an elderly man laughed at my youthful optimism. 'Semi-final, ha!' he said as if I had suggested that the Left might go along with the nuclear deal.

Still, as India stumbled and sailed through, Kapil Dev making more than 80 out of that 175 while I was driving on a Lambretta from home to the local Doordarshan studio, nobody believed India could win. Indeed on the evening of the 25th we had a little school reunion planned. I saw the first half of the match at a friend's place in colour (they were the only family I knew who had colour television!) and then popped off to Nanking in Secunderabad, absolutely certain that the game would be over before the mandatory sweetcorn vegetable soup arrived. We only discovered that the West Indians had lost 7 wickets when a friend called home and by the time we reached his house, Kapil Dev had got Andy Roberts lbw.

In the month that followed, Doordarshan must have played that match every day. I swear I could have told you what was going to happen with every ball, and every time Kapil Dev ran backwards to catch Viv Richards, we celebrated. Soon, rewards were being announced with the kind of fanfare that suggested 1947 had arrived again. Land was being promised, so were rice and railway tickets, and then, like now, it gave crooked patriots an opportunity to get into the newspapers by making promises they never intended to keep anyway.

So did India win that day or did the West Indies lose? Were the mighty champions overconfident? Or did a group of honest triers get it right just when it mattered?

I guess there is merit in the overconfidence theory as there is in the fact that India caught everything that came their way and had the bowlers for the situation. But remember too, that it was a wonderfully balanced team with five seam and swing bowlers and one spinner and virtually no tail-ender. Kapil Dev batted at no. 6 but the next three (Kirti Azad, Roger Binny and Madan Lal) could have played, and indeed did, as batsmen for their state side. Kirmani had batted no. 7 for India in Test cricket and Sandhu had to be one of the stodgiest no. 11s around.

Twenty-five years later, World Cup '83 was an example of what was possible. India didn't have even the pockets of affluence and enterprise it does now and the win appeared as a ray of optimism. A day after India became World Champions, I boarded a train from Hyderabad for Ahmedabad, a journey that took thirty-six hours and a day's stop over in Mumbai to complete. A few months later, in a classroom, a professor was wondering whether India would have a 1000-crore company. Twenty-four years later, a television company paid four times that for rights to a T20 tournament!

But for all the changes since, try telling me that there has been a greater moment in Indian cricket.

THE NEW, MELLOWED DHONI IS THE SMART PLAYER TEAM INDIA NEEDED

29 August 2008

There is a sense of calm that you experience with Mahendra Singh Dhoni that you don't with say, an Amar Singh or a Mamata Banerjee. He isn't a rioter anymore, though he often batted like one in his baptism years. Now he has grown, he has mellowed, he has become constructive and yet the target is the same. He is more the clinical assassin, taking in the situation, surveying the landscape and waiting for the moment, aware that it can be his. There isn't the sense of drama, no Bolt, no Isinbayeva, no Ronaldo—gee, more Bindra,* really.

And this might sound strange, but he actually reminds me of how Rahul Dravid used to finish matches in his

---

On 27 August 2008, M.S. Dhoni scored a match-winning 71 at Colombo to take India to an ODI series victory against Sri Lanka.

*Abhinav Bindra, who won the first ever individual gold medal for India at the 2008 Olympics, in shooting.

74

glory years of one-day cricket, 2002–05, when he carved fields rather than lambasted them. He gave you the impression that there was a run-rate chart in his head. Dhoni does so too, not quite in the erudite, elegant manner that Dravid possessed but in a street-smart, worldly-wise manner: a jab here, a cut there and always a great sense of the two, the most productive shot in the game. It is a very long time since I have seen a wicketkeeper, even as strongly built as he is, run like Dhoni.

And much like Dravid at one end caused Yuvraj and Kaif to play their finest one-day innings at the other, so too does Dhoni inspire confidence and I have no doubt that the mature innings the frustratingly brilliant Suresh Raina played at the Premadasa had something to do with his partner. Dhoni doesn't always speak of his methods, his mindset, which is a bit of a pity, because he is now an ideal lesson in how to grow as a cricketer. But worryingly for this side, there isn't another finisher of the same pedigree and that often means he has to time his charge rather too precisely, sometimes even giving the impression he is holding back too long. So then, what position does he bat at?

For too long, Dhoni believed no. 6 was his slot but his current move to no. 5 is just about ideal. In the absence of an in-form Tendulkar or Sehwag, he is currently India's best limited-overs player and quite the best in the middle overs. I thought the manner in which he handled Ajantha Mendis was excellent. He wasn't always reading him, but by playing late and getting maximum value from the nudges and flicks he was able to generate, he limited the threat of Mendis and set India up for the end overs. Sport always values the smart players—not always the show ponies, not always the bugle-blowing marauders, but always the smart players. Dhoni is the smart player India needed.

As a captain, I suspect he has got away with playing a

bowler short. It was a tactic Sourav Ganguly used with some success during India's fine run in 2002–03, but it always placed a great burden on the four bowlers picked. If one of them had a bad day, there was no one to turn to. I guess positive captains don't think like that, but Dhoni would clearly like another bowling option and that is what makes Sehwag so crucial to this line-up. With Sehwag and Tendulkar in the side, strange as it may seem, it actually allows India to play seven batsmen, even though six batsmen and Pathan should do.

Irfan, though, remains the enigma, the perfect link player in the Indian team; the one man who can give it the balance that would make it complete. But I suspect even Dhoni is losing a bit of faith in his bowling. From a distance, impressions can be wrong and this one hopefully is, but it does raise the question of what Pathan's continued role is. If he regards himself as an all-rounder, it allows him to justify a place in the side in spite of a poor bowling performance in case he gets runs. He can believe he is pulling his weight in the side even if it comes at the expense of his primary skill. So the question for Indian cricket is: do we look upon Pathan as a bowler and let him recognize his great skill again, or do we look upon him as a no. 7 batsman who may or may not bowl 10 overs?

It is an important call and it is one that Dhoni must take sooner rather than later.

MULTI-DIMENSIONAL PLAYERS ARE NOW A NECESSITY, NOT A LUXURY

5 December 2008

Cricket continues to prove, as it has for a while now, that teams need multi-skilled players. That can sometimes be interpreted to mean bits-and-pieces players. It can be a fatal misinterpretation. Those players have rarely made a contribution to one-day cricket. Instead, what I am suggesting are players who have substantial skills in one area of the game, good enough to earn them a place for that alone, but who then contribute significantly in another area. Ricky Ponting with his fielding is an example, so is Sehwag with his off breaks.

Very often such potentially valuable second skills tend to get ignored, or under-worked. With the kind of schedules players have these days, it is tempting to train your primary skill and if fielding is the second skill, then do a bit more work there. The time to develop another skill is, I suspect, when a particular player has a break or while the others might be playing another version. Clearly you need

This piece was written soon after India won its ODI series against England at home 5–0.

77

a dedicated facility for this and luckily, India now has a very nice one in Bangalore with a fine coach and support staff. The National Cricket Academy (NCA) under Dave Whatmore could, additionally, develop a specialized skills programme, a custom-made programme for specific cricketers.

Let me give you an example. India are playing Yusuf Pathan at no. 7 and really, the only reason they can play him is because they are a fairly complete side with ten players. And Pathan is no more than a 3 or 4 overs bowler at this level since he doesn't really rip his off breaks. However if he could become a better off-spinner, then he would provide greater variety to his captain and make a stronger case for his inclusion in the side. Now, when the rest of the team is playing a Test match, which he is currently not required to play, he could spend a week at the academy with a coach who will work on his off breaks, show him newer skills and he could practise them for as long as he wanted. Then, armed with this knowledge he could bowl better in the nets and thereafter, in crunch situations for his team.

Someone like Robin Uthappa, for example, who has done a fair bit of wicketkeeping as a young man could, likewise, spend a week training with a wicketkeeper and developing a second skill. He would, probably, never be picked as a second wicketkeeper but in case he was in the side and the regular man went down, the team would have someone to turn to. For Uthappa, this would be an opportunity to provide a better basket of skills to the selectors and the captain.

I'd recommend we go further and hold a batting camp for bowlers. We all know what happens during the nets. The batsmen bat and the bowlers bowl and when the time comes for the bowlers to get a hit, the batsmen are fooling around with the ball and dishing up the kind of stuff that will never be bowled in a match. And so the bowlers, already inadequate with the bat, never get to improve. They don't need to average 20 with the bat, but hang around and make 10 or 15 and help 30 or 40 get added to the team score. At one level, people like Munaf Patel and Ishant Sharma need to learn; at another people like Piyush Chawla, who can bat, can aim towards becoming all-rounders.

This development of a second skill has long been practised by good companies who, for example, get excellent software engineers to learn communication skills which will come in handy later on in their careers. I believe cricket is ripe for such specialized second-skills coaching. It might have been a hindrance all along when the academy didn't have either the desire or the manpower to do anything significant. Now, we can and this will go a long way in producing more rounded cricketers. If India seeks to dominate world cricket, it needs to produce cricketers who can do more.

The climate is right at the moment; India has a fairly young side that if nurtured could dominate world cricket. A second skill must be mandatory and the NCA can become a pivotal resource in ensuring that. This is a wonderful phase and it comes rarely. This is the time to be innovative, to arm our talent better.

WITHOUT FEAR, VIRU'S COME INTO HIS OWN

13 March 2009

It would be easy to image Virender Sehwag as a pirate, terrifying genteel passengers on a cruise liner with his weapons and his audacity. Picture the bandana, the cutlass coming down with the speed of a bat clobbering a ball past mid-on! Pity then that he has the look of a genial halwai* from Chandni Chowk, chubby cheeks and an enduring tussle with his girth, enjoying his jalebis as much as he does serving them; never too far from a smile and, as we now know, from the odd wink as well!

New Zealand's bowlers might think he is a bully, riding roughshod over them and trivializing their offerings. But he isn't a bully either because all bullies are, inherently, cowards shying away when someone bigger comes along. Over the last eight years, Sehwag has taken on the quickest

---

In the Hamilton ODI against New Zealand on 11 March 2009, Sehwag blasted an unbeaten 125 off 74 balls to lead India to a 10-wicket victory.

*Sweet-maker.

in demanding circumstances and sometimes he has won and sometimes he has lost. But he is willing to take on the bowlers and the conditions, not afraid to lose, and that is not a quality bullies possess!

There is a secret to his fearlessness, a trait that resides in all those who are happy to live with risk; or indeed risk as most of us perceive it. Sehwag is not afraid of getting out. It doesn't mean he is lackadaisical or that batting is a reckless, momentary pursuit. It is just that his mind is free from the fear of defeat.

And as most of us would have seen in our own lives, the moment we contemplate defeat, we open our doors to it. I'm sure he is aware, like most of us are, that in the pursuit of success, failure is always a neighbour, a bystander waiting to jump in. But the more we look sideways at this neighbour, the less we look ahead. Sehwag has this extraordinary ability to let failure jump in from time to time but not worry too much about it.

But then, he has always been like this. What explains this amazing burst, this transformation from a potentially great but terribly ordinary one-day batsman to one that bowlers around the world fear and who, in his last twenty games, averages 60 with a strike rate of 130? For years Sehwag was a huge under-achiever, averaging a mere 30 at the top of the order and possessed of a maddening urge to find the fielder at third man to a ball that was short and outside off stump. Now he hardly seems to get out there and surely it cannot be because bowlers have stopped bouncing it short and high outside his off stump? Is speed, or lack of it, the issue, or are bowlers indeed bowling fuller, or is there a greater discretion in his stroke play?

My guess is that he now has a greater variety of shots, especially on the leg side. He always flicked the ball well off his pads but could be kept quiet by the ball that bounced into his ribcage. Now he seems to have a couple of shots for balls in that area. First, the trademark straight jab through midwicket, a shot achieved through his incredible bat speed. But more important, when it gets higher, he has started pulling the short ball. And anything that comes off the middle of the bat and achieves decent elevation goes out of the ground in New Zealand anyway!

I also suspect he is being given the space that every performer needs. Inherently, performers need to be happy souls—a trapeze artist worrying about his job will probably find the safety net. With Gambhir, Yuvraj and Raina batting well, Dhoni solid and reliable and Tendulkar still evergreen, Sehwag probably has the licence to play his brand of fearless cricket. And he seems to be carrying this freedom with a touch of gravity because it can be a thin line between bravery and recklessness. For Sehwag to find out how far his ability can take him, he must have the freedom to play in his style, and this team, through its composition and attitude, is giving him this freedom.

And so Sehwag can embellish our game with his own brand of cricket; so different from the two greats of this era—Rahul Dravid and Sachin Tendulkar. Dravid is the kind who would study angles like a draftsman, work out the best ones to employ and then use his incredible work ethic to perfect them. Tendulkar, for all his genius, has never been independent of the field setting, either showing up gaps through his placement or creating them where he wants to by playing the ball elsewhere (see how he plays the paddle sweep which forces a fielder to be placed there and opens up a gap where he wants it to be opened).

But Sehwag looks upon the field placement as an independent event—something the opposition captain has to do but not anything he needs to worry about.

That is why it is a great game; because it has room for all kinds; and because it has room for Sehwag.

DON'T WRITE OFF ONE-DAYERS JUST YET

11 September 2009

I suspect the only entity that's got bashed around as much in recent times as the one-day international is the villain in the Hindi film (who, intriguingly, often gets flattened by a size zero heroine as well). Reading some of the stuff you would have thought we were talking of crossbows and log tables and bats with linseed oil! So are we at a tipping point; is the gathering momentum weighty enough or is there too much fluff in it; are we merely filling newspaper space because we have to?

I'd rather wait and see what the Champions' Trophy, another much maligned format that is going through a makeover, throws up. With just eight teams, well, seven, and a nationwide poll to find people who can bat and bowl making up the eighth, it offers much by way of competition. Sambit Bal, the editor of Cricinfo is right. You need to look at things in a certain context and the

---

This piece was written soon after Sachin Tendulkar famously supported the suggestion that ODIs should feature two innings of twenty-five overs each per side.

Champions' Trophy in this format provides that context. It separates it from the otherwise wild mushrooming of one-day internationals.

Shorn of their context, one-day games are a weaker offering. Put in the right ambience, they could be thrilling. It is a bit like the great violinist being ignored when he plays outside a subway station but being flattered with expensive tickets and applause when he plays in a theatre. Before writing an obituary we need to give the patient a good shot at survival.

Having said that, though, the debate has thrown up a few interesting thoughts. Matthew Hayden thinks the middle overs, widely seen as the weak link, are actually the most interesting, since they test a player's skills greatly. And Peter Roebuck thinks we bring the problem onto ourselves by setting deep, defensive fields and making the single easy and attractive in the middle overs. It is an argument worth looking at. Why don't captains attack a bit more after the power plays are over? In most games fielders are pushed back as soon as allowable; it's as predictable as people responding to a fire alarm or a commentator throwing to a break! The moment you let ordinary bowlers bowl to ordinary fields, you get ordinary cricket. That is why the new power play rules are so good. They force captains to keep the fielders in, then, perforce, to attack. So here's another theory. Attacking captains will bring the zing back into one-day cricket.

The other idea, now much discussed, is to split the game into two innings of twenty-five overs each. We need to be careful while accepting or rejecting this, since we need to know the reason for the suggestion in the first place. If the idea is merely to spice up the game and see more big hitting, then this is not too different from playing two back-to-back T20 games. With a lead and a deficit it has enough variables, and a few things to commend it, but essentially it is T20 wearing a disguise. If, on the other hand, it is to ensure that both teams play under similar conditions, which I think was the basis behind Sachin Tendulkar's suggestion, then we need to carry over the score. Take a break after 25 overs but then get the same batsmen out again and treat it like a 50-over game. That would require a greater degree of traditional skill and retain the difference between formats.

BEYOND THE WORLD CUP LIES THE FUTURE OF THE FORMAT ITSELF

28 January 2011

There is more at stake than who wins the World Cup when it presents itself before the cheering masses on our subcontinent. People have begun to wonder, with a mixture of concern and excitement, whether the home team can indeed win it. In both India and Sri Lanka the answer is yes, and in Bangladesh they can, for the first time, be genuinely optimistic about doing more than merely making up the numbers. But beyond that lies the question of the future of the format itself. If the World Cup is the pinnacle of the one-day international, it has to be a roaring success for the format to have an assured future. It hasn't been in recent times.

The World Cup in the West Indies* was insipid, hardly a word anyone could have dreamed of using with respect

This piece was written a few weeks before the beginning of the 2011 Cricket World Cup, which was jointly hosted by India, Sri Lanka and Bangladesh.

*The previous edition, held in 2007

to cricket in the Caribbean. Since then, there have been good games and bad, large crowds and empty stands, and now there is further proof coming in from Australia that if the context is right, the 50-over game is right, but if it isn't, not many people are interested.

The first four one-day games* have been the dessert after the main course that the Ashes was, not the guest that doesn't leave until the lights are shut off. The Ashes were wonderful, but the fear was that both the players and the spectators would be exhausted by the tension of it all. Not true. Stadiums have been full and viewership has been outstanding. So too with the one-dayers between India and South Africa. It would seem that the one-day international still has much left in the tank.

However, where the action has not involved two fancied teams, or those with a long established rivalry, television rights holders have seen their investment pummelled, and entering grounds in some places has been a bit like going to a restaurant that has fallen on hard times. It would seem to reaffirm the hypothesis rapidly gaining ground that it isn't the format but the quality of the competition that seems to count.

It is against this background that the World Cup comes to the subcontinent, needing a balm after the injuries of the last edition, but also seeking a confirmation of its value to the cricket-playing world. Will the context, so obviously relevant, pull viewers and spectators in? Or will only some games attract notice, leaving the seemingly lesser ones, of which there are plenty, bereft of attention? Ecuador vs Switzerland at the FIFA World Cup would pull in many more viewers than it would if it were a mere friendly. Will South Africa vs Netherlands manage that?

---

*Between England and Australia

If indeed the viewership and attendance tend to be too strongly skewed, if games not involving the top four of five leave people disenchanted, it would mean that the ICC decision to have no more than ten teams for the 2015 World Cup is right. It would also ask some rather uncomfortable questions about cricket's huge investment in becoming a global sport. I do believe that, as the parent body, the ICC must do its best to allow everyone in the world to play cricket—the emergence of Afghanistan has been one of the most touching things to have happened—but if teams don't compete, that investment will need to be questioned.

Kenya is a good example. Eight years after making the semi-final, even though it required a fortuitous turn of events, their cricket is going downhill rapidly. Ireland made an impact in 2007, now the world will want to see their progress. Otherwise, it will be tempting to go back to the everyone-plays-everyone format of the 1992 World Cup.

It is important too that India, Bangladesh and Sri Lanka put on a real show. While the faithful will throng the stadiums anyway, the right ambience and buzz can draw in the sceptics. In recent times the news from outside the field has been discouraging, and cricket itself hasn't always taken centre-stage. Fans need to be proud of their World Cup, and it won't help if scaffoldings are up in stadiums in the month in which the tournament starts. The World Cup didn't creep up on us.

Happily though, winter has started running out of steam rather quickly in the last week. While it means temperatures might be higher, it could also limit the effect of the dew, which can ruin a contest. A hot World Cup on hard, dry outfields might not be great for bowlers, but if the fans like the runs scored, it might serve a greater purpose!

AS THE MERCURY RISES, EXPECT SPINNERS TO TURN ON THE HEAT

11 March 2011

Winter, or what we had of it, is saying goodbye, and the World Cup is scrubbing itself clean of its influence. The second half will be quite different, and teams will have to gear up to the newer challenges on the way. Pitches will start getting drier and outfields quicker, and players will discover that their intake of fluids has increased steadily.

It probably means that spin will have a greater role to play, even more than it currently has. Already, throwing the ball to a slow bowler in the power plays, once considered a surprise, a fad, is becoming normal. It is a strange game; the spinners are bowling the new ball and the quicks are waiting for the shine to go off a bit. It's all happening, Bill Lawry might say.

We saw first signs of that with M.S. Dhoni giving Ashish Nehra only one over with the new ball against the Netherlands. Zaheer Khan got three and by the sixth over

---

The first round of the 2011 Cricket World Cup featured forty-two matches and was played over thirty days. This piece was written with ten days of the first round still waiting to be played.

there was spin at both ends. Being able to cut and pull and stand up to pace are no longer qualities you need from an opening batsman. More interestingly, around the twenty-eighth over, both were back, this time to get the ball to swing the other way (by the way, which is the right way now?) before it was changed after the thirty-fourth over.

Indeed, as pitches get drier, the surfaces get more abrasive, and the ball will swing the other way quicker. Already, the slow-motion cameras are showing little bits of leather coming off the ball within ten overs; I won't be surprised if we start seeing more of that. It means teams will need more bowlers who can take the pace off the ball, and already teams are adapting. The mighty South Africans, they of the muscular hit-the-deck variety of bowling, have played three spinners. In one of their games they had Botha, Peterson and Imran Tahir plus du Plessis, Duminy and Graeme Smith himself to turn to. Old warhorses must be spluttering into their Castles* at the sight.

Only Australia, among all the teams at the World Cup, are sticking to their guns, and they have some big cannons. It is not a contrarian view but one that they have thoughtfully opted for. When bowlers can bowl fast in the air, it doesn't really matter how slow the tracks are, and they have picked genuinely fast bowlers. It helps them overcome the drought they are facing with spin bowlers. They could have come to the World Cup with more reliable but slower bowlers, but that would have been fraught with danger. This is not a medium-pacer's tournament.

The heat will affect them, but the team that has the most questions to answer with the bowling is India. In a couple of matches, significantly, against weaker teams,

---

*A famous brand of South African beer

Yuvraj Singh has been able to gloss over the shortcomings, but on flat decks against strong batting sides India's bowling will look very inadequate. I won't be surprised if the track at the Chinnaswamy was the last batting paradise that India will play on. Expect slow, low surfaces where the ball will grip a bit.

The need to have slow bowlers using the new ball in the power plays will impact India's selection policy too. Yusuf Pathan cannot be a regular in the early overs and Dhoni would dearly like Harbhajan to play as a wicket-taker in the middle overs. You don't need to be too intelligent to deduce that it means R. Ashwin, happy to use the new ball, must play. It also means that Piyush Chawla must make way and that is where Dhoni's selections have baffled many.

I wonder sometimes if the fact that he wanted Chawla in the first place is causing him to try and prove a point. That can happen if the captain goes out on a limb and insists on a player and keeps playing him to justify the original selection. I can't help thinking, though, that Dhoni is too clever a captain to do that and maybe he wants to keep Ashwin away from the other teams and throw him in as a surprise. We'll know soon, but Chawla cannot complain he didn't have the captain's faith.

It is going to be a week of jostling for positions, and once the two points are in the bag it will be a question of getting that net run rate up.

CONFIDENCE SKY-HIGH, INDIA HAVE EDGE OVER LANKA

1 April 2011

The two best teams in the tournament, and by no coincidence led by the two finest captains, will contest the final—nothing can be better for what has been an outstanding event. The World Cup has given new life to the 50-over game, and it has been hosted with great passion in Bangladesh, Sri Lanka and in India. Now, it has a dream final.

India will start favourites because they seem the more rounded of the two sides; they have players for most occasions and they have batting match-winners of extraordinary pedigree. More important, as the tournament draws to a close, they seem to have a better idea of the combination that they must believe will bring the World Cup home.

Sehwag and Tendulkar are the best opening pair of the tournament, though, by sheer weight of runs; Tharanga and Dilshan will contest that. After the 175 against

India played Sri Lanka in the final of the 2011 Cricket World Cup on 2 April 2011.

Bangladesh, Sehwag has been playing cameos, a bit like a brilliant actor working two shifts and having to leave quickly after having delivered his lines impeccably. But even if he only does that, he makes it much easier for the batsmen to follow; he especially takes the load off Tendulkar who, apart from a quixotic phase in the semi-final, is batting as well as he ever has. The one thing he doesn't have in his gallery, a winner's medal, is one step away and I will be very interested in seeing how he keeps ambition at arm's length in the final!

India have resolved what is becoming a key position at this World Cup with Suresh Raina batting with much confidence against both Australia and Pakistan. Truly, he has won back his spot, and it has been wonderful to see him field, excelling in an area India is rather thinly endowed with. And Dhoni's extraordinary handling of Yuvraj Singh means he has the option of playing an extra seamer as he did against Pakistan. By working on his bowling, Yuvraj has given himself the time to rediscover his batting form, paradoxical as that might seem!

India will come to Mumbai with their confidence soaring after back-to-back wins against opponents with whom they have had their most bruising encounters.* And I have no doubt that Dhoni will not allow a win against Pakistan to be rated higher than any other. It cannot be so. It was a semi-final, not a final. Indeed, Dhoni's leadership has been outstanding.

He has backed his hunches, taken calls that might have seemed bizarre at the moment, but at all times he has stayed calm, in control. It is a wonderful quality for a leader to possess. Having taken India to a World T20 and

---

*India beat Australia in the quarter-final and Pakistan in the semi-final.

to the number one spot in Test cricket, he now has the opportunity of winning a World Cup.

Arrayed in front of him are Kumara Sangakkara's mild, humble men who become mighty competitors on a cricket ground. They have the most wonderfully innovative bowlers, men with unique styles and actions and who come at you from different angles. The top four batsmen are in brilliant form and like India, they are led by a man with extraordinary poise and assurance. Unlike India though, they haven't quite ticked off all their boxes yet.

Dilshan, Tharanga and Sangakkara have batted with great assurance but after them, Jayawardene, another big match player, hasn't had enough time in the middle and nos. 5, 6 and 7 appear a bit fragile. I believe Angelo Mathews should be the highest of those numbers, but he seemed to be in some pain in the quarter-final. If he is handicapped, and cannot bowl, for example, the Sri Lankans will lose the one outstanding feature they possess: the balance to the side. Mathews must bowl, for otherwise the bowlers would start occupying positions from no. 7, and that would be dangerous. It must be a worry too that neither Samaraweera nor Silva have looked in good form. They look vulnerable if someone can penetrate their excellent top order early.

Hopefully, Murali will be ready for the big day. He has had an extraordinary sense of drama to his life, picking up wickets with the last ball he bowled in tests and in one-dayers in his country. Winning a World Cup and retiring would be a dream come true. In the home dressing room too, they will be aware that the best present they can give Tendulkar is a World Cup medal. There will be some emotion that day in both camps.

Hopefully it will be a match worthy of a final, but, even if it isn't, and the last three haven't, it will not take away from what has been a really good World Cup.

TESTS

KUMBLE REPRESENTS THE BEST OF TEST CRICKET

7 October 2004

A monument was built and a seed was sown and both were thrilling to watch. One man showed why the word 'great' sits humbly on his shoulders, another suggested that it might one day accompany him. And after all the doubts over the series, and the maddening possibilities, Test cricket gave its devotees their fill yet again. After three insipid one-day tournaments, this series is already starting to show that maybe it is one-day cricket that needs those oxygen cylinders.

Anil Kumble is the repository of a lot of fine, traditional virtues. He is a simple man who works hard and if that doesn't earn him too many commercials, he won't lose sleep over it. It has been a wonderful journey and, happily, the destination doesn't seem to present itself just yet.

At various times in his career, it has been pointed out

In the first Test against Australia in Bangalore in October 2004, Anil Kumble overtook Kapil Dev's record of 434 wickets to become the highest wicket-taker for India in Tests. The immensely talented Michael Clarke made his debut in the same Test.

to him and he has faced it stoically. And he has rarely been undignified. Some of these virtues are considered boring but they stand the test of time. He has made an epic and, long after the thirty-seconders are gone, we will remember this.

Fourteen years ago, a shy man in glasses and without a passport was first picked for India. He was an unlikely looking spinner, over six feet tall with the delivery stride of a fast bowler and he didn't turn the ball much. It is a good quality to have but as he has happily shown it is not the only one. A huge heart, control over length, variation of pace and a terrific attitude count for much more. That is the legacy for young men who seek the end and undermine the process.

And it could so easily have been different. His first tour was followed by a year and a half in the wilderness which he wisely used to become an engineer and then set about scripting a great home record for India. The nineties belonged to him and to Sachin Tendulkar, not just to one of them—and if India felt proud of itself, if the crowds thronged to Test matches, it was because Kumble was skittling out the opposition consistently.

He didn't loop it like Prasanna, curl it like Subhash Gupte, tease a player like Bishan Bedi did, but he took wickets. Sometimes we can put too much store on form and far too little on content.

I am delighted for Kumble because I have been an unabashed fan and I stood up and applauded today and I hope all of you did as well. It is a monument he, and all of us, can be extremely proud of. The landmark of 434 will fall as most things must with the passage of time and maybe 500 beckons but I don't think he will be thinking about that today. I think he will be wondering how he can win this Test for India and that would be typical of him.

One day Michael Clarke will have a monument against his name too. He has many summers ahead of him, and the odd winter, but the seed of a fine career was sown today. I might be sticking my neck out but I think we can tell another generation that we saw Michael Clarke make his Test debut.

CHAOS THEORY:
COMPROMISE + MYOPIA = IDENTITY CRISIS

I remember sitting in trigonometry classes many years ago and being occasionally stumped by identities: those questions where you are given the left hand side and the right side of an equation and have to provide a proof (something like: prove that [cosecA − sinA] [secA − cosA] [tanA + cotA] = 1)!

They seemed easy because you knew where you had to get to in the end. And so we bumbled and bulldozed our way through, often creating new laws of trigonometry on the way. It wasn't always good enough because it was the path, the procedure, that mattered, not the end we knew.

India's selectors found themselves in a similar quandary when they picked the team for the first Test. They knew the right hand side of the problem (pick Ganguly!) but weren't quite sure of the process that would get them there. And so I'm afraid they have bumbled and bulldozed

After being stripped of the captaincy and dropped from the team, Sourav Ganguly was picked for the Test squad to tour Sri Lanka in December 2005 as an 'all-rounder'.

their way through as well. Their solution is neither elegant nor correct.

Producers of films face similar problems too and come up with a solution that works for them. When they have a star with a small role to play, he cannot be top of the credits nor can he, of course, be the third or fourth name. Some get by with a 'guest appearance' or 'special appearance' but my favourite is where the title sequence reaches a climax, the music, the drums reach a crescendo, the screen goes momentarily blank and then suddenly gets filled with: 'and above all, Dharmendra!'

India's selectors seemed to have done that; picked fourteen and 'above all, Sourav Ganguly'.

It needn't have been that way. Ganguly isn't a young man with a hint of promise in his kit bag. His game is an open book, he's made 5000 runs at a decent average of 41 and, until he got waylaid a bit by the frills of his job, was a mighty fine player.

The desertion of focus, unlike hair loss, is not an irreversible process and it could be argued that Ganguly might still get it back. That is the kind of judgement selectors are expected to make, they are allowed a qualitative input, even a hunch where the statisticians are required to be imprisoned by hard numbers. Both have a role to play and neither can play each other's.

Accordingly, I would have admired the selectors if they had said that, having been out of the team, they believed Ganguly would be hungry and that they felt they owed a very fine player that opportunity. Some might have disagreed with that opinion, we are all entitled to that, but it would have been an opinion born out of conviction. It would have meant leaving out either Yuvraj or Kaif, a hard call, but that is part of a selector's job.

Instead the selectors have stooped to compromise, they

have embraced that vicious enemy of excellence and initiative. They have picked a player for the wrong reason and, by trying to justify it, are looking in need of a hiding place.

The same committee that was bringing in fresh air has succumbed. They have displayed their weakness by calling Ganguly a 'bowling all-rounder' or a 'batting all-rounder' or both. They could have called him a reserve wicketkeeper and wouldn't have been much further off reality. The last time we heard something as funny was when Shane Warne said he took a diuretic because his mother asked him to.

Sourav Ganguly has always been a batsman who could bowl a bit and he will play the first Test as just that, no more, for India cannot play six batsmen, a wicketkeeper, Ganguly and three bowlers. Asking him now to be anything else is being unfair to a person who has done wonderful deeds for Indian cricket.

Ganguly is a tough cricketer, he has faced challenges before and he has another in front of him. All sportsmen go through that and Ganguly must approach it proudly. By having unnecessary tags attached to him, he is being put through greater pressure than he needs. I am not sure he has the best friends at the moment. They seek to bring him in through the back door when, as a proud and fine cricketer, he should be blasting the front door open. He's been down that path as well.

The last couple of days are suggestive of the chaos that surrounds us. We often talk of finding a way through it and, indeed, clever leaders generate chaos so that no one else can navigate. But the problem with chaos is that it doesn't recognize patterns. There was a very good one emerging in our cricket. Pity about the past tense, hopefully for the time being.

As a long-time admirer of Ganguly's and the spirit he

brought to Indian cricket, I must confess I am very keen to see him do well. But he must walk in through the front door as one of India's six best batsmen, not be made to slink in with another name tag on his chest.

NOBODY STOOD OUT AND THAT IS WHY INDIA WON. CAN THEY DO IT AGAIN?

17 August 2007

A number and two pictures summed up this series for me.

On the final morning we were looking at India's performances overseas and two captains stood out. Sourav Ganguly had won eleven away Tests and Rahul Dravid five. Both had more away wins than losses. No other Indian captain came close to achieving parity. And it struck me how beautifully the baton has been transferred from one man to another.

They might seem to be different people. Ganguly, bold, flamboyant, in your face and passionate about winning. Dravid, studious, reserved, polite and passionate about winning. You might wonder about that last expression in the light of his defensive approach in the second innings at the Oval. But he was trying to win, in this case the series not as much as the Test. And more of that later! But isn't

---

In the summer of 2007, Rahul Dravid led India to a series win in England. India drew the last Test at the Oval to win the series.

it amazing how the same expression can sit easily on the personality profile of both these remarkable men?

And so to the first picture. Dravid and Ganguly embracing at Trent Bridge after the last run had ticked over. Two men, born to walk on divergent paths and yet in their common passion for Indian cricket, producing astonishingly parallel careers. It was fitting that the two were together in a moment of victory. Dravid had given everything he had to his captain and now Ganguly has returned the compliment. How much nonsense has been written and said about those two!

The second picture. India have just been presented the winner's trophy. Even Dravid, not averse to a jig these days, was ebullient. Somewhere in that crowd of smiling faces, Kumble might have permitted himself one too, for it is not like him to seek out the front row. But there was a man, a child you might think from his expression, holding that trophy with the joy usually reserved for your first-born. There is little that Sachin Tendulkar hasn't done in this game, including playing the unfamiliar dour innings, but look at that picture and you will feel this is the first time he has played for India. I found it deeply moving.

And so a team written off won a series; not by some astonishing deeds of valour—there was no boy standing on the burning deck, no charge of the light brigade, no Aamir Khan in *Lagaan*. This was not the India of individual stars, of prettiness and fragilility. It was about Dhoni, the inveterate racer willing to drive in first gear and stop at traffic lights, it was about V.V.S. Laxman the painter playing a steel-maker. It was about two openers hanging in there and denying the new ball a wicket. Nobody stood out and that is why India won. Can they do it again, I wonder?

Still, it would be easy, but misleading, to conclude that

India are now a team of steel. They have done it once or twice, the foundries do it every day. Catches are still going down and the fielding has the flavour of lethargy to it. But hopefully the message will have gone out. It is cohesion and the commitment to the good of the team that wins matches. Maybe coalition partners can learn that as well.

There were two leadership qualities that stood out for me as well. Dravid, a person and a cricketer I have always admired, showed enormous integrity and humility. And by his statements at the end of the match he rose even higher in everyone's esteem. It is not for nothing that he is regarded as one of the statesmen of the modern game. If he was sitting in his drawing room and watching the game he would have been frustrated too at the decision to bat again, he said, and in doing so he offered respect, not sullenness, to those who criticized him. It is a rare quality. But he knew something we didn't know, he said, and so he bit his lip and took the decision that he thought was best for his side. We have a right to disagree, as he admitted, but the intent was honourable.

And he admitted he batted poorly. If it was painful for you to watch, he said, can you imagine how painful it was to play it? There was no attempt at justification, no suggestion that the situation demanded it, just an acceptance that it was an off day. Luckily for him Ganguly played a brilliant cameo, as good as any you will see, and took the pressure away. Deservedly, Zaheer Khan was man of the series, but Ganguly would have earned a special mention. He continues an astonishing comeback, now back to being silken and flowing, unrecognizable from the fidgety, stumbling batsman of 2005. The laugh is back, even the hair is back, and the runs are back. Maybe the break was good after all!

This is quite the most appropriate Independence Day

gift. We are now sixty, young, vibrant and confident. And if our politicians can put country first, like these young men have in this series, we will win more. Vande Mataram.

SLOWER, LOWER PITCHES ARE A CONCERN

30 November 2007

'Wives,' Navjot Sidhu once said in a style only he can get away with, 'are like pitches. You never know which way they will turn!' I wonder if women are more entitled to feel that way about husbands but even if we stick with the original Sidhuism, my experience, and that of many friends, suggests wives are far more predictable and reliable. For a long time now, we've been hearing from captains and groundsmen, and many other sages, about pitches in India and about how they are going to crumble and turn and the only point of debate seems to be when rather than if. But more often than not, pitches are getting slower and lower and flatter and seem to bind better as the game goes on.

One person who would know that better than anyone else is Anil Kumble. Through the nineties, he demolished teams on pitches that crumbled and offered uneven bounce and he knows that doesn't happen too often now. And so he would take such comments, in his usual stoic manner,

Anil Kumble became India's Test captain with the first Test against Pakistan in Delhi in 2007–08.

with a pinch of salt and just move on. However, the fact that our pitches get increasingly slower and help neither batsman nor bowler produce attractive cricket is a matter of concern. Like pre-election announcements, meant to be heard rather than believed, we keep hearing of how our pitches will be redone to produce better cricket. Now, Daljit Singh* is saying something similar and I hope we can recall optimism from the ruins it lies under.

One Test is probably too early to judge Kumble as captain. He has made some fine moves and set some good fields but his best moment actually came a day before the Delhi Test when he said V.V.S. Laxman would play. Kumble has been a hardworking cricketer and understands that nobody likes uncertainty for it merely festers negative thought. It would have been unfair to let fine players like Laxman go to bed on the eve of an important match not sure of whether or not they will play. It has been done before and the less frequent it is the better it is. Laxman responded with a classy knock and if that surprised people maybe they are watching the wrong game!

Now, people feel the need to react similarly about another fine and gutsy player. Since he began opening the innings, Dinesh Karthik has hardly ever failed. For a man not yet twenty-three, he has been shunted all over the order and in the field, has faced more uncertainty than a stockbroker and has inevitably responded with good cheer and great attitude. He is not prone to making wild statements and, let's face it, is performing a role that more pedigreed players were not too keen on. Openers have to be persevered with, you don't throw a fresh lot in every time, and that means riding the trough from time to time.

---

*Curator of the Mohali stadium, arguably India's best cricket ground.

For Yuvraj Singh* it means going to first-class cricket and scoring a potful of runs. Honestly, I don't know what he was doing in Delhi when he could have been playing for Punjab and, if he has no role to play with bat or ball in Kolkata, he must insist on leaving and playing a Ranji Trophy match. A big, and more important, long innings in the middle will do his case no harm so that when the time comes, as it inevitably will, he will be ready.

Yuvraj is one of the few to have emerged from Robin Singh's† report with flying colours. Indeed, he remains as sharp as ever and hits the stumps better than almost anyone else in world cricket. But someone needs to be worried about why Robin's report is in the media and what it means to future reports he might want to, or have to, write. The routine leaking of information from the BCCI is something they need to worry about but currently all the action seems to focus on the trivial. The Vengsarkar issue‡ was a small matter; a smart organization would have ticked it off a things-to-do list in no time at all. When the trivial begins to occupy time there is little left for the crucial.

If Indian cricket, and its attendant arms, has to waste time talking and writing about a selector's column, we are in deeper trouble than we care to admit. And I'm told the search for the coach is giving high-budget reality shows a few jitters!

---

*Yuvraj was not in the playing eleven.

†India's fielding coach.

‡A spat between Dilip Vengsarkar, chairman of the selection board, and the BCCI, over a cricket column written by the former.

DON'T WORRY ABOUT TEST CRICKET, IT'S IN THE PINK OF HEALTH

9 January 2009

Once again two rivals, with a history of bad blood between them, have shown us up to be a community of hypochondriacs. We fret over Test cricket, we dissect it, we search for the smallest sign of weakness to pronounce illness and once again we have been shown up.

Test cricket is robust and, as we were taught to say by high school teachers, in the pink of health. We don't need to protect it, merely educate another generation. We worry too much.

Yes, there are trends as owners of television channels will tell you. Yes, more people are watching T20 but bell-bottoms came and went and came back again. Test cricket will never compete against T20 as fine dining cannot against the hamburger. But children are still learning classical music. In less than a month we have had three stirring

---

The final Test of the series between Australia and South Africa in Sydney, which Australia won, produced one of the most gripping finishes Test cricket has seen.

games, heartwarming displays of character, skill and bravery. They talk about the golden age of cricket. If it was better than this month all I'll say is they had better cricket writers!

For an hour and a half at the Sydney Cricket Ground, on a pitch where one ball kept low and the other leapt at you, nos 10 and 11 for South Africa kept Australia's bowlers at bay. On skill and ability alone they had no business to be there that long. But those are tiny adjectives when placed alongside mightier ones like determination and tenacity. Dale Steyn and Makhaya Ntini would have been pardoned for being out twice each in that much time. But the opponents had to be denied even if victory was impossible. And Steyn and Ntini denied Australia for an hour and a half. In doing so they showed that every player must have a second skill, however tiny, and be prepared to use it as armour.

Then Graeme Smith walked in. A proud, tough but increasingly genial man. He shouldn't have, but sport produces such characters. A bad leading elbow and a broken left hand meant going to the toilet would have been bad enough. Putting on a glove would have been a nightmare. But he was prepared to walk in to face two bowlers bowling at more than 140 kilometres an hour. With all your limbs and all your faculties available it is a challenge. And he blocked and he blocked till a nasty one crept through a fairly limp bat. Australia had won, but so had South Africa. I can't think of another game, other than life, where saving the day can be so exhilarating and heroic.

It is moments such as those that Steyn and Ntini and Smith encountered that show up the kind of person you truly are. When the going is good almost everyone can swim with the tide but it is when confronted by adversity that character emerges; or, as Warren Buffett said, when the tide goes out you know who has been swimming naked. Smith's decision to bat was brave, courageous, some might say foolhardy, but he would have slept well at night knowing he had given the team everything he had. And he can now ask it of his team. In an era of political manoeuvering and lying, missiles and rockets and killing and corporate hoodwinking, it seems a pretty noble thing to do.

Soon the two teams will resume battle on another continent. Playing away is a greater challenge and Australia will have to show they are up to it. It is a wonderful concept we must have more of. After six Test matches, with each side having encountered home and away conditions, we will know which is the better team. It seems a fair and challenging way of going about things, a welcome change from the two-Test nonsense some have to endure.

Thereafter we in India will be in the grip of T20 cricket with first the IPL and then the rest of the world joining in for the World Championship. It will be great fun but it will not demand of its warriors the challenges that Test cricket does, with fast bowlers bowling as many overs as they like on a fifth day pitch against tail-enders. And there will be no glory in blocking. It will demand different skills, different qualities and will produce different drama but it would be folly to compare the two forms. We must have both.

WITH BATSMEN LIKE SEHWAG, IT'S ALWAYS ALL OR NOTHING

3 April 2009

Exhibit One is shortish, tubbyish, balding and very very Delhi. Exhibit Two is tall, lean, muscular, a rebellious South African in English colours. Intriguingly, they have a very similar approach to the game. Few other cricketers can pull in as many people to watch a cricket match and then have them on the edge of their seat all day. Virender Sehwag seems to hit the cover off every ball and yet his last eleven Test hundreds have each been in excess of 150. Kevin Pietersen seeks to impose himself on the game every ball and isn't too far away from the odd daft shot but no one, apart from the Don, got to 4000 Test runs faster. For two people who carry a self-destruct button as closely as a terrorist would a cyanide capsule, they have crafted extraordinary careers.

Sehwag has embraced risk the way a seeker does his faith. Or maybe we have been looking at risk differently over the years. That is what the pioneers do; they question

---

This piece was written towards the end of India's victorious 2009 tour of New Zealand.

established thought. It is an approach that has worked exceptionally well with him and indeed, now defines him as a person. And yet, every few innings we moan over his choice of shots, we exhort him to be more judicious; we tear our hair out in frustration. We want bits of Sehwag, not the whole person, almost as if he were a roast chicken and we could choose the parts we wanted. We can't. With Sehwag, as with everyone else really, we buy into the whole person, into the package. If it isn't acceptable, we discard the package—but we cannot pick and choose.

And so we want him to play that incredible fourth innings 83 against England at Chennai, in a very small shortlist of his best performances, but can't fathom his shot when India have to bat two days and a bit to save a Test match. We want it both ways; some days we want him to cut loose and gape at him when he does, and at others we want him to bat two days and scream at him if he doesn't. We cannot accept that fact that he is different, that if he is told not to get out he won't score a run.

It would be an easy, if slightly boring, world if everyone could be the way we wanted them to be. 'Sehwag, bat two days to save this Test!', 'Manmohan Singh, erect statues of yourself in every city!', 'Fardeen Khan, act!' Life would be a beautiful buffet but it isn't. If you are chasing a target Sehwag is your man, if you want someone to bat for your life, get Rahul Dravid. You need both. If we ask them to be different, we get a different person!

So too it is with Kevin Pietersen who is all aggression, all ego, all 'Pietersen-centric' as the English media now refers to his view of the world. Why can't he be a bit different at times, they ask. A little more discreet maybe? A little more correct, a little more, what shall we say, acceptable? Appropriate? Effectively, we are asking, why can't he be a bit more like Andrew Strauss sometimes?

Doesn't Strauss come from South Africa as well? So then . . .?

The ego, the aggression, the latent lack of belonging and the consequent larger-than-life portrayal define Pietersen. That is how he is. He will play a breathtaking innings one moment and shoot his mouth off the next, but that is the package we buy into.

As journalists, commentators, or just observers, we are often called upon to comment on people's performances. And very often, in our minds, we create this perfect entity: the dash of Sehwag, the composure of Tendulkar, the patience of Dravid, the dignity of Laxman, the elegance of Ganguly. Indeed we create God himself and arrayed against this epitome of perfection we search for shortcomings. Sehwag shouldn't have played that ball, Dravid should have stepped on it earlier, Laxman should have moved his feet more . . .

Maybe we should accept people for who they are, indeed for what they are; for the basket of skills they bring to the table and therefore for the deficiencies that are a part of them. Like us, but on a wider screen maybe, they will succeed and they will fail. Because that is who they are.

INDIA'S NO.1 RANKING MUST BE
SEEN WITH A SENSE OF HISTORY

11 December 2009

India have not set foot on the summit by stepping off a helicopter, they have got there after establishing several base camps and making steady, sometimes hazardous, progress. India's ascent is not a point, it is the current status of a curve; it is not a moment in time but part of a phase. Any attempt to think otherwise would be unfair and shortsighted.

And so while India must celebrate, it must be with a sense of history. This lot of players have put the ribbon on the box but the cake was baked by many; they have scored a goal but you cannot do so unless someone has passed the ball to you. And that is why the only aspect of this moment that disturbs me is the cash award to this team. I am not a huge fan of cash awards to professional players, they are presumably paid to win anyway, but this announcement ignores the fact that various others set it up over the last five years.

In December 2009, after defeating Sri Lanka, India became the no.1 Test team in the world.

In particular, India have been served by three very fine captains before the hugely impressive current incumbent. Very few good teams win with inadequate leaders anyway. Under Sourav Ganguly, India realized that winning overseas was an option and India have much to thank a player the world found very convenient to misunderstand. Rahul Dravid was the perfect captain to follow with his strong commitment to the team and to the cause. It is easily forgotten that under him India won in the West Indies for the first time in thirty-five years and in England for the first time in twenty-one. And Anil Kumble was the leader at a decisive moment in Indian cricket, in Australia in 2008, where the Test win in Perth must rank as significant as the win at Kolkata in 2001.

Don't forget too that Mahendra Singh Dhoni's current record reads played 10, won 7, lost 0. Included in that is a series win against Australia, an away win in New Zealand and now another against Sri Lanka. There are no freebies there. Something is right in Indian cricket.

Indeed, India's current position is good for world cricket, as indeed South Africa's little reign at the top was. Three teams competing for number one is always better for the sport than a giant blocking everyone's path. But I am a little concerned at the state of denial in some parts of the world, with the difficulty in acknowledging this, with the continued devaluation of India winning in India not accompanied by a similar status to Australia winning at home or for that matter South Africa or England. India's winning streak has not been due to financial jugglery, which is a convenient myth in itself, but due to good cricket. To assign other reasons, and what a pity that is being attempted, is to undermine players of extraordinary pedigree.

And these are not just batsmen. True, Sehwag, Gambhir,

Dravid, Tendulkar, Laxman, Ganguly, Yuvraj and Dhoni (even Jaffer and Karthik at key moments) are extraordinary players and they have set up many victories, but to focus on them would be unfair to those who take 20 wickets. Against England, home and away, Zaheer Khan was player of the series; against Australia it was the very impressive Ishant Sharma who will soon be leading India's attack again. Amit Mishra and Sreesanth have had their moments in the sun, and Harbhajan has taken more wickets than many of us think he has.

But, as with all success, India must celebrate the moment and move on. Australia and South Africa are fine teams, and Sri Lanka have just the man to drive their transition. And, as business leaders will tell you, it is more difficult to stay on top than to get there. India need to groom batting replacements, and there are only two on the horizon, the scarcely tested Murali Vijay and the untested Cheteshwar Pujara. Harbhajan Singh desperately needs competition to take him to another level, but, more important, India will have to find a way to ensure that players of serious ability like Rohit Sharma, Sreesanth, Ishant Sharma and R.P. Singh don't lose their way. And it will call for people with vision at the top. They exist, but they are in a bit of a melee at the moment with others of various hues and political colour.

Isn't it ironic though that, for a country accused of devaluing the game, India are struggling in T20 cricket but are atop the summit of the most traditional form of the game? Maybe there is a story there.

TEST CRICKET DYING? NOT IF YOU LOOK BACK AT THE DECADE GONE BY

25 December 2009

Like a Hollywood studio production line, doomsday scripts are deluging us. But as we know scripts can be scary; they need not necessarily be true. And so it must be stated upfront: cricket is not in peril; it is merely undergoing change. Some people equate the two, but that happens every time a comfortable world order is disturbed. Cricket as we knew it might change, but that has also happened with the way we communicate, with the way our families are structured and with the kind of medicines we take. Change doesn't always mean progress, but the status quo isn't always the best result either. It is merely the most convenient.

The decade started with one of the greatest Test series of all time when Australia came to India in 2001. At its midpoint we had one of the most riveting Ashes series ever.

This piece was written in the last week of the first decade of the new millennium.

And the decade ended with some quality cricket between Australia and South Africa, and Pakistan and New Zealand, another fine Ashes series and a contentious Indian tour of Australia where controversy shrouds the fact that it was still an excellent contest. Notice Australia is the common factor, and, even if some of their cricketers believe that laws concerning behaviour should be a bit different for them, it cannot hide the fact that they produce the best cricket on the planet.

Elsewhere, in the middle of the decade, cricket caught politicians napping and brought Indians and Pakistanis closer than ever before. But politics had the last laugh and that wonderful period between Kargil* and Mumbai's 26/11† may never return. Cricket's greater enemy, certainly in our part of the world, is not change but the hatred that evil minds spread and feed on. Don't forget, too, that cricket gave South Africa one of its most-loved icons and allowed Makhaya Ntini to script one of sport's nicest feel-good stories.

And so, in spite of being on death row for a while, Test cricket gave us many happy moments this decade. And, given its resilience, it would be fair to expect a few more in the decade ahead. The key question, though, will be whether or not youngsters either want to play it or look upon it as the highest form of the game. Those that lit up this decade, the Warnes and McGraths, Pontings and Tendulkars, and Dravids and Muralis grew up dreaming of playing Test matches. Teenagers today may not feel the same way and by 2015 the T20 generation will be playing international cricket. That will present an interesting challenge.

---

*May–July 1999

†November 2008

Already we are seeing fewer and fewer cricketers wanting to bowl quick. And it is the best way to sneak into a world eleven of Test cricketers at the moment! Even Shane Bond has quit, Shoaib Akhtar is a memory, Dale Steyn turns up far too infrequently, Brett Lee looks like he is done, Fidel Edwards is occasionally sighted, Kemar Roach is too young for an assessment and Ishant Sharma is as confused as young men his age tend to be. That explains the number of 50+ batting averages in recent times and also why it has been a batting decade.

The good old one-day international has been knocked around a bit too but viewership figures and attendances seem to tell a story that's a bit different from that which some columnists have been propagating. My suspicion is, as I argued sometime back, that it is not the ODI that is in danger, but the world contest played in front of neutral audiences. There is so much cricket that viewers must prioritize, and so home games are doing well and others are being ignored. If that is what market research is telling us then we need to tailor our products accordingly. The World Cup of 2011 is consequently going to be a key event in shaping the future of cricket contests and one that the ICC must watch very closely, since they will be impacted the most.

The end of the decade was lit up by the IPL and T20, by the arrival of the brash young kid. To be honest I am not worried by that since most nonconformists are labelled brash anyway! And it is the nonconformists that challenge the world not those that seek satisfaction in the status quo. It has given the consumer what he or she likes and has given many more players the opportunity to earn a living from the game. We'll wait and see if it becomes a monster or a saviour!

And so it has not been a decade of doom, merely one of change.

IN SEARCH OF A SECOND WIND

8 November 2010

By playing with a bat Michael Hussey called 'three metres wide', and doing so in his thirty-eighth year, Sachin Tendulkar doesn't only continue to give people a hard time, he gives hope to many others that if you stay around long enough a second wind is possible. Of course it assumes that you will be picked in that period—some teams cull ruthlessly while others enforce temporary bans—and be fit enough to scour the horizon for that second coming.

I thought of that as I saw Rahul Dravid struggle his way through his first hundred balls in Ahmedabad. My mind, so full of admiration for a great cricketer, was willing him on, but younger, more irreverent observers on my Twitter feed were calling for his head. Apart from a little purple patch in 2009, he was averaging in the thirties over three years (interestingly these numbers are very similar to those Tendulkar generated during his lean phase

---

In November 2010, Rahul Dravid scored a difficult 104 in the first Test against New Zealand at Ahmedabad—his thirtieth Test century.

123

in the middle of this decade) and wasn't always looking like the great player he is.

Surely on a cruelly flat deck and against an attack that wasn't likely to scare a top team, he could have batted like the player we knew, or indeed like the player we saw after the shackles he had imposed on himself were broken and a century appeared! Or was it that Dravid was building bunkers around him, creating defences against every possible dismissal? Was he getting so caught up with survival that not getting out would seem a success?

A couple of days earlier I had heard Sourav Ganguly say, on a news channel, that as a player moves past the mid-thirties he loses his confidence far more than he loses his ability. And I wondered if that was the case with Dravid, surrounded as he is by young batsmen who admire him but challenge him nonetheless! Was he so increasingly aware of his mortality, I wondered, that he was guarding himself against every possibility?

Sometimes players, like managers, can analyse in such detail that they end up thinking of weaknesses that may or may not exist; batsmen can start preparing for every possible way in which they can get out. As patients get older, they worry about infections cropping up from just about anywhere whereas in younger days they might have drunk water out of the tap at a railway station or jumped off a tree oblivious to injury. Batsmen can, therefore, start focusing too much on not getting out rather than on scoring runs.

Indeed, watching cricket in that phase you couldn't help thinking that one player, Sehwag, was looking for an opportunity to score while another, Dravid, was searching for safety. Virender Sehwag scored a free-flowing 173 in the same innings. One seemed to enjoy being out in the middle like a kid might on a roller coaster while the other was gritting his teeth like he were preparing for an assignment on the implications of Bernoulli's Principle. (And given that the passage of a ball through air tends to be governed by the work of the aforementioned gentleman, he probably wasn't too far away anyway!)

Having said that, Dravid could well counter the point that he has addressed every match the same way in the last fourteen years and has an extraordinary body of work to support his thesis, that on another day Sehwag might look flippant and the gravitas that Dravid exudes might be more reassuring, that being a man of erudition, a deep thinker and an analyst has always worked for him.

As it turned out, a century duly arrived, one that took him past Bradman's twenty-nine, once considered as unattainable as a four-minute mile was, at a strike rate better than that achieved over his career. The second half of his innings, in terms of balls faced, produced 80 per cent of his runs. The certainty that Dravid exuded through a glittering career was back, the feet had started to glide and the bat was searching for runs where it had been intent on guarding the wicket.

Did the confidence that Ganguly was talking about return? Did a voice tell him that putting money in a locker was not much good in a bull market? And will this century, and the accompanying confidence, lead to the second wind, the kind Tendulkar has shown?

I do not know. But what I do know is that beyond a point, the more you analyse the more you budget for failure. Now that may be good for Obama's security entourage but not necessarily so for quality cricketers.

SACHIN'S BRILLIANCE SHADOWED INDIA'S FIRST-TEST WOES

24 December 2010

Sachin Tendulkar has made a fiftieth Test century seem more like an appointment kept than a journey into the uncharted. Great men do that; reaching out to things that others cannot even spot. His longevity has been staggering and I often wonder if others deny themselves that option because they stifle the child within, draining out the enthusiasm that an untroubled childhood possesses. Tendulkar's fiftieth, and in course of time maybe his hundredth, is as much a tribute to his innate ability and extraordinary intelligence as it is to his youthful exuberance. Cricket is a toy, a pet, that he hasn't yet outgrown.

Too many others fall in love with the reward; in its mindless pursuit they find the journey tedious; they seek to shorten it, often to ignore it. It has become clichéd to say so but Tendulkar is still in love with the journey. The box

---

In the first Test at Centurion against South Africa in December 2010, Sachin Tendulkar scored an unbeaten 111—his fiftieth Test century. India lost the match.

office may pass its verdict but the role is still to be enjoyed. It's an extraordinary, beautiful way to live, and one that is available to all of us!

But Tendulkar's fiftieth, dazzling as it was, blinded many to two other events. In an extraordinary, and dare I say heartless, act of omission, most of India chose to ignore that another legend of the modern game had gone past twelve thousand runs. Rahul Dravid has rarely demanded the spotlight and, increasingly, in India, with its modern obsession for self-promotion, the strong, quiet, efficient ones get overlooked.

If Tendulkar's life is about enthusiasm, Dravid's is about determination. If Tendulkar is the child splashing colour with glee, Dravid is the scientist in relentless search for progress. Dravid might seem weighed down, but that is his style and it is a style that has served him and his team handsomely for almost fifteen years. Tendulkar might have been a Formula One driver or a striker in a goalmouth; Dravid would have been an Olympic shooter.

Twelve thousand runs is a colossal achievement; very good players are respected for life for scoring half as many. It is a reward for an unwavering work ethic, for a man who has never drifted from the path of perseverance and integrity—two rather unfashionable qualities in public life these days. By not recognizing the magnitude of what Dravid has achieved, India has let itself down.

Having said that, neither champion would have enjoyed the occasion. Indeed, Tendulkar's achievement blinded many to the fact that a Test match was eventually conceded; once again, India had lost the first Test overseas and, once again, the lesson will be completely ignored.

India are slow starters on bouncy pitches. It takes time to make the adjustment, even for the very best; as it would be for a linguist speaking Tamil for a couple of years to switch to French immediately. But India have always been adamant about not giving themselves more than a game to acclimatize; now even that is a luxury. And so, we must reap what we sow. In 2007 in England, rain, and an astonishing umpiring error, allowed India to escape with a draw in the first Test and in Australia later that year, India kept the tradition alive by losing the Boxing Day Test match.

Yet India seem to enjoy jumping off planes and into cricket matches. In 2007, after much pleading, Anil Kumble was given one warm-up game in Australia. I found that staggering; that an Indian captain was having to negotiate with his own administration for the best possible opportunity to win. Admittedly, there are some players who don't enjoy playing warm-up games on the grounds that they are served with poor opposition on pitches that may not always resemble those in Test matches. And it is true that conditions at Centurion on the first day were very different from those on subsequent days, but I can't help thinking that better preparation might have ensured India didn't get bowled out.

But India's current problems lie deeper. The best teams in the world are those that are capable of taking 20 wickets in most conditions. Strong bowling sides keep you in the game longer than strong batting sides do. India's bowling at Centurion was amiable, even embarrassing; it didn't have the potency to drag India back into the game and allow the second innings performance to take them to safety. India might have lost the Test on the first day, but the bowlers ensured that no other result was possible.

India produced the landmarks, brilliant as they are; South Africa produced the result.

INDIA'S BATTING IS AGEING, BUT ONLY ON PAPER

31 December 2010

When the mighty fall it's news, and nothing quite said it for me in 2010 as well as Australia's dramatic downfall did. They were expected to go into decline, but not quite into disintegration. The Aussies are normally the chin-up chest-out variety of mankind, but a succession of defeats tests even the mightiest of spirits. Australia's confidence plummeted—they are not as bad as they look—a state of mind they have induced in the opposition, but rarely experienced themselves.

Interestingly, the replacements of the greats aren't quite there yet. To some extent that is understandable, if they were easily replaced the greats wouldn't be regarded that way, but their first-class cricket isn't throwing up tough, sound players. Marcus North was a battler but, if he was representative of the middle-order strength of Sheffield

---

After losing their no.1 ranking the previous year, Australia had a terrible year in 2010. India, South Africa and England emerged as the top three Test teams by the end of the year.

Shield cricket, there is a little more trouble on the way. Brad Hodge's interview was the strongest statement by a middle-order player in the year!

Australia did two very un-Australian things in the year. One, they assumed the Ashes were lost with three to play. And I wondered what battlers who wore the coat of arms, with the kangaroo and the emu, two species that cannot take a backward step, had to say about that.

And two, they lived in the past, what with all the exhortations to Warne to make a comeback. One of the things I have always admired about the Aussies is that they always looked to make the best of a situation and not lose too much sleep wondering why they got there. Maybe the behaviour patterns of people low on confidence are identical across cultures!

Australia's downturn coincided with England playing their best since I started following cricket. English cricket has rarely symbolized steel; there have been some tough individual cricketers but collectively they tended to talk better than they fought. They produced outstanding cricket writing—rarely outstanding cricket. But now there is steel here. I don't know how much of it was Duncan Fletcher's* doing but I have long admired Andy Flower, who has been the perfect coach; his influence has been felt but he has rarely been seen or heard. And England didn't mind picking tough but understated cricketers like Jonathan Trott, who has been quite an unsung hero for them.

England's resurgence makes for a good three-way tie at the top of the table. From the demographics you might think that India have seen their best cricket with a lot of ageing stars around, while England look to be on the way up and should fancy having a real crack at number one.

---

*England's previous coach

The best balance though, in spite of losing the last Test of the decade, probably exists in South Africa. Jacques Kallis has been their player of the decade, probably their best ever, and the only all-rounder in world cricket. His exit, when it comes, will be a blow that will test them.

India's batting is ageing, but only on paper; otherwise, like good wine, it is getting better, certainly with Tendulkar and V.V.S. Laxman. And surely it should escape nobody's attention that Dravid had a huge century two Tests ago. For India to hang on to this position, they need Zaheer Khan to be fit and on the ground, for he seems to catalyse India's younger bowlers, some of whom are vanishing as quickly as they come. It is a worry and a threat, a bigger threat than that posed by franchises and commissioners, which occupy administrative minds for much longer.

While the top four of five teams are playing, Test cricket seems safe, even vibrant. But five teams cannot sustain a game, and the descent, towards the latter half of the decade, of New Zealand and Pakistan will add to the threat. Already the West Indies are being buffeted: by poor quality and the inability of the administration to prevent players from missing Test cricket for 20-over cricket. Theirs will be a long climb up, if indeed there is a climb.

Pakistan represented the tragedy of the decade. Leadership and vision are the problem there, and that seems far more difficult to find than mesmerizing bowlers or attacking batsmen who keep jumping off buses. We thought that the absence of international cricket on home grounds would be a challenge, but keeping the structure together seems tougher. The fixing saga hurt people but didn't surprise them and, while the ICC does its best to keep their finances afloat, the real initiative must come from within. They must make news on the field, not around it.

The decade ahead will test all forms of the game: Test cricket for its longevity and relevance to a new generation, one-day cricket for its very survival and T20 for its sustenance. But in the land of its birth, in its traditional opposition, in Africa and in the financial nerve centre people still want to watch it. It is a good way to start a new decade.

CRICKETING GREATS

THE PRO AND THE PRODIGY

10 September 2004

There would seem to be little in common between the worldly-wise experienced pro just named the best player of the year and the bubbly young man who is the finest nineteen-year-old cricketer in the world today.

One is a middle-order batsman with extraordinary powers of self-denial, standing like a wall against the best bowlers in the world; defying them, even hurting them. The other is a bowler, just out of adolescence, just becoming aware of what a reputation is. One is erudite, fancies a musical, reads heavy tomes, speaks to managers. To the other, life beyond the movement of a cricket ball is neither exciting enough, nor indeed apparent.

One grew up in a middle-class but comfortable family where academics was perceived to be the path towards an honourable existence. The other grew up in a relatively poorer, deeply religious environment where God and the service of the faithful were paramount.

In 2004, Rahul Dravid was named ICC Player of the Year. Irfan Pathan was named Emerging Player of the Year at the same awards.

And yet Rahul Dravid and Irfan Pathan have much in common; nature's extraordinary ability to grant similar attributes to those plucked from different forests. They are both soft-spoken but deeply ambitious, they don't strut and are very respectful of age and achievement, but more than anything else they seek to learn and to improve. In a gurukul they would have made excellent shishyas!

I remember watching, first with amusement and then with satisfaction, Irfan Pathan staring at Wasim Akram, unable to take his eyes off the great man, cajoling him, pestering him to teach him another ball. The yorker was discussed, the slower ball explained and the merits of bowling straighter when the ball didn't swing gone into.

Each discussion was followed by an experiment: on the field of play and against the mighty Aussies. This young man wasn't afraid of being wrong, of an embarrassing attempt, and because of that he had the greatest chance of succeeding.

And suddenly I remembered another young man, slightly older at twenty-three, but only two Test matches old, at a dinner in Toronto where the first Sahara Cup was being held. Ian Chappell was one of our commentators and, as a man who loves the game deeply, he was never far from an interesting conversation.

There was a crowd around him and on the fringe was young Rahul Dravid, his neck thrust forward like a little child who doesn't want to miss out on the news. As the crowd thinned, he grew bold to ask a few questions himself. Dinner was secondary, for him and for Chappell. It was the first time I had seen him do it. It hasn't been the last.

Now these two men, possessors of dignity and a smile, have new challenges ahead of them. Travel and fatigue are appearing on Sachin Tendulkar's body and in the next couple of months Rahul Dravid will have to move up to playing Tendulkar in the side. He has played that role already, only it hasn't been called that.

Amid all the talent around him, he will have be the one looked up to; his presence at the crease a sign of calm, his departure the signal for butterflies to flutter. It needn't be that way but that is how we follow cricket, we like to deposit our hopes on individuals much like we do on our gods.

Tendulkar has done that since he can remember and it is this ability to play with the burden of others' expectations that makes him one of the game's immortals. Dravid will feel that should Tendulkar's elbow fail to heal.

And Pathan will have to keep brushing that halo away when he runs in to bowl, for while India will rejoice in it, and keep replenishing it (if one can do that to a halo!), it matters little to Australian batsmen. An award and more money than he could have imagined ten months ago can produce pride and pain depending on whether they are embraced or kept at arm's length.

Both will continue to knock at his door should he bowl the ball in the right places and maybe, add another yard of pace. Speed isn't everything—the resurgence of Chaminda Vaas and the continued excellence of Shaun Pollock are proof of that—but, if he can start nudging 140 kmph, he will have added that little extra zing.

One of Dravid's greatest strengths has been the ability to keep his feet on the ground. Pathan has it as well.

As you can see, they have much in common.

THE BIG EASY

25 March 2005

Inzamam-ul-Haq reminds me of a banyan tree: huge, immovable, cool, soothing, roots everywhere you see; roots that can slow you down or roots that can provide strength. There is a timelessness about him that makes urgency seem an irrelevant fetish. And yet he also reminds me of a sitar player who plucks each string carefully, each motion designed to produce a specific piece of music, every note in place and unhurried; occasionally glancing at the tabalchi, giving him a moment and moving on.

He's not the prancing guitarist, no extraordinary flurry of activity to produce a short, breathtaking burst of music. He's unlikely to say 'aah, baby' everytime a word eludes him. The world needs those too, only they were born elsewhere, where the wind had several appointments to keep in a day.

In Inzamam's house, the wind comes to stay, produces a couple of delicate zephyrs, curls its way round and lingers over its goodbye. In Inzamam's world the child can

---

This piece was written soon after Inzamam-ul-Haq became captain of the Pakistan team.

138

come charging in saying '*Abbu, Abbu, dekhiye to kya ho raha hai*'* and he would listen carefully and say '*Acchha, zara chai khatam karke dekh lete hain. Arre bhai woh biskut kahan gaya.*'† That kind of world!

And now it is hard to imagine that Inzamam came into world cricket as a destroyer. He played an extraordinary New Zealand side, for whom the whole had a ridiculous exponential relation to the sum of the parts, twice in a few days in the 1992 World Cup and broke as many hearts as is possible in a country of such few. Suddenly the world was watching him and listening to Imran Khan, the finest picker of talent in the game. We were in Australia before the World Cup when Imran's opinion on a relatively unknown Inzamam became known. Then, like now, he found creative ways of getting run-out and people had begun to wonder if Imran had played a mind game by throwing in this lumbering young giant. He was to justify his captain's faith, like Wasim and Waqar did. It's not a bad trio, that, and who knows Imran as prime minister might discover a similar defence, finance and home minister!

But this lumbering giant had another quality. He had eyes that spotted things before a predator, a trickster or a politician could. He was a great judge of length and pace and so seemed to have all the time against bowlers when others seemed to be as much in haste as a just-departed train.

And word began filtering through that the best player against Waqar and Wasim in their prime was Inzamam in the nets.

---

*'Dad, Dad, just see what's going on!'

†'Ok, let's just finish our tea, and we'll go see. Hey, you, what happened to those biscuits?'

His laidback style seemed to push the headlines away. And so while the world talked of Tendulkar and Mark Waugh, of an emerging Lara and in course of time of an emerging Ponting, there wasn't the same flurry of adjectives with Inzamam. Two years after that World Cup I saw him decimate New Zealand again at Sharjah and he was as brutal as his style would allow him to be. It wasn't just a flat deck and a reluctant attack, it was a batsman who wore the cloak of majesty.

Now he is captain and must be seen to be here, there and everywhere on the field. He must dart between press conferences, interviews, practice sessions, selection committee meetings and barbs from volatile teammates.

These are not slings and arrows, for Inzamam they seem to be mines and missiles and clearly he does not enjoy them. He is a reluctant leader of men for he must then escape his world and embrace another. When the little child runs in and says '*Abbu, Abbu, dekhiye to kya ho raha hai*' he must bound out of his chair and say '*Chalo dekhte hain abhi*'.*

To be captain of Pakistan is to be permanently on the war-front, to be a Chengis Khan or a Mahmud of Ghazni. Inzamam is more Bahadur Shah Zafar, to whom the ghazal was more important than the cannon. His dynasty had seen Babar and Aurangzeb, only the occasional Shah Jahan, but the last Mughal emperor was more likely to go into battle saying '*Wah bhai Zauq, ek aur sher sunaen*'† or '*Miyan Ghalib, is jang ke baare me aapki kalam kya kehti hai?*'‡

---

*'Let's go and see right away!'

†'Mr Zauq, let us have one more poem.'

‡'Dear Ghalib, what do your books have to say about this war?'

But unlike Bahadur Shah Zafar, who wasn't much of a warrior and ended up being imprisoned, Inzamam can bat. He won't be imprisoned, and he has been one of the highlights of his era and this series.

LIFE SEEMS EASY WHEN YOU'RE IN THE ZONE

1 April 2005

There comes a time in the life of some sportsmen, only some, and it rarely comes more than once, when they believe they can do anything, even fly; when the idea of being vanquished is a distant, lonely world that strange beings inhabit; when the mind ceases to comprehend fear and when confidence breaches its barriers and flies forth into audacity without even recognizing it. They call it being 'in the zone' and no drug has taken man there, for this is the lovely, unscripted real world.

In course of time a player steps down from that pedestal, indeed is made to by this strange unending reality show, and then looks back and gasps at what he has done. He cannot take himself there again but is forever condemned to being seen in that heavenly light.

All of a sudden the ball that he dismissed from his presence is an object to be respected, the mind starts

---

In the Bangalore Test against Pakistan, Virender Sehwag hit a double hundred off 262 balls, while Sachin Tendulkar laboured to 16 in 140 minutes before getting out. India lost the match.

conjuring possibilities that it wasn't required to imagine in that state.

Sachin Tendulkar has lived in both worlds, Virender Sehwag has yet to make that journey. He believes he can fly.

And so Sehwag cannot understand why Tendulkar, a player of infinite possibilities, one he hadn't dreamed of sitting beside let alone batting alongside, is playing a mundane game while he himself kisses the breathtaking.

In course of time Sehwag too shall descend and live with the mortals and another young twenty-two-year-old will wonder why. Those 'in the zone' are ruled by instinct, those that descend must see and embrace reason and caution.

That is why Sehwag believed the Bangalore Test could be won in much the manner that Tendulkar was the only man on the planet who was even contemplating a win in Sharjah in 1998 when the rest were happy with scoring just enough to qualify.*

Tendulkar is at a different stage in his cricketing life-cycle. He is not coming to the end, not just yet, but he has become respectful; in a manner of speaking, behaving with the bat like he does off the field as a brother, father or a dear friend might.

It is this embrace of reason, this grip of caution that surely caused him to play one of the most uneventful innings of his life in Bangalore. When on song, Tendulkar

---

*In one of the most famous ODIs of all time, India were chasing Australia's 284 in Sharjah in 1998, needing to score 237 in 46 overs to qualify for the final on net run rate, which they did, thanks to a superb innings from Tendulkar. To everyone's surprise, Tendulkar kept going, aiming for victory, and almost got there, scoring a blistering 143 off 131 balls.

is a very misleading player to watch for he gives the impression there is nothing wrong with either the pitch or the conditions, indeed that there is little right with the bowling.

At Bangalore he must have convinced most into thinking that this was the same surface from 1986 and that Warne was bowling at one end and Muralitharan at the other. Five Test matches before this one he walked out onto a treacherous surface at the Wankhede Stadium and made it obey his command. Those that had seen that innings from the dressing room would have thought the pitch was fine, just as at Bangalore they would have been convinced that it was unplayable.

It is all in the mind. The surgeon that can find his way through a maze of capillaries must one day wonder how to go past an artery; Lata Mangeshkar must listen to *Mughal-e-Azam* and gasp.

But Tendulkar needn't be there yet. You can't help thinking though that he chooses to be, that he writes a script ahead of its time, that he looks at himself in a crystal ball and snatches the future. In all fairness he only does that sometimes, he averaged around 50 for the series, but when he does you want to tell him to let the future take its course.

Meanwhile, Sehwag plays the most breathtaking cricket of his life, his mind unburdened by any thought other than the shortest line between his bat and the boundary. His batting is simple, he draws bold strokes on his canvas, and he is free of anxiety, the greatest worry that can befall a performer. India is letting him down for he is creating time for the bowlers and seeing it used up by the rest of the batting—a very gifted line-up that is chained by worry and anxiety and self-doubt.

This is the moment Sehwag must contribute the most

to the side off the field as well; carry his unbelievable joie-de-vivre everywhere and unlock doors for Ganguly and Laxman, two fine seagulls meant to fly high and gracefully but having to squabble for runs.

Their problems lie, like with so many others, in that most beautiful and complicated arena, clothed in simplicity one day and indecipherable on another. It is in the mind that all the battles must be fought: Sehwag's and Tendulkar's, Ganguly's and Laxman's.

THE TORNADO WITH CALM
IN HIS EYE

20 January 2006

Virender Sehwag and Rahul Dravid. A tornado and a sea-breeze, a raging river and a calm ocean. How utterly incredible that two people with such differing style and manner should be masters of the same activity!

Sehwag continues to astonish and to redefine the role of the opener; a slot once occupied by the likes of Hutton, Boycott, Gavaskar and Turner to whom taking the shine off the ball was a slow, meticulous affair. They laid the foundation, they famously gave the first hour to the bowler, they practised denial. If you dangled a deliciously evil dark chocolate outside Gavaskar's off-stump, he would ignore it.

More recently that job has gone to a Hayden, a Gayle and a Gibbs. And a Sehwag. None of them believe too much in elaborate footwork and patience is a dated virtue to them.

But even here Sehwag stands out for his amazing ability to stay inside the line of the ball and free his

Virender Sehwag said famously in an interview that he had no idea who Vinoo Mankad was.

shoulders. The text book, a bible to some but a mere thriller to him, would have him move across to cover his stumps, get his body behind the line of the ball and play along the ground in front of the wicket. Instead he stays on leg stump and backs himself to hit through the line of the ball and often, even to carve it with an angled bat. Very few openers in the game, as gifted as him, would create a V between third man and extra cover, ninety degrees away from its original location!

It is a style that requires its owner to possess the manner of a gambler; willing to flirt with danger at all times, not retreat to safety after initial success and to forget the last bad throw of the dice. Dravid couldn't be one. He would work out probabilities and conclude that the odds weren't worthwhile. He would get behind the line of the ball!

But it is precisely Sehwag's ability to forget the previous delivery, even laugh it away, that is his greatest strength. To worry about the previous ball, the earlier innings, is to be the owner of a cluttered mind; thinking not of the ball on the way but the impact another one has had and this one could have.

To Sehwag, every ball seems a fresh offering, a new game; the earlier ball, like the spoken word, gone forever. It is a refreshing philosophy but one only few can practise.

And how arrogantly he dismisses a ball from his presence. Like the cruel zamindars in the movies might a worker or a booking counter clerk in the railways might you or me!

Dravid will study the offering, work out his response and in the act of doing so, give it respect. He is like the musician plucking each note carefully, a scientist doing a titration where each drop matters. Sehwag might wonder at the need for it.

But don't ever let this apparent lack of studiousness lull you into thinking that, like a three-shift actor, he merely turns up on the sets and asks for his lines. Few people in the game see the ball as early as Sehwag, few make up their mind as quickly, few have a quicker grasp of what the ball is likely to do.

And he isn't a sparkler either, producing a blaze of light and smoke and getting extinguished. A hundred runs to him doesn't seem to be a major destination, just another number that someone else is keen to record. And so there is no release of energy when he gets there, no need to take fresh guard, no need to refocus; he gives the impression he is waving at the hundred as he drives by. Hence the big centuries.

Hence, too, the comparison with two other players of our time who too are quite happy to be alongside the ball rather than behind it and who, more often than not, dispatch it breathtakingly to the boundary. Brian Lara and Adam Gilchrist, now sadly a little short on runs, are equally thrilling and carry this delightful air of unpredictability.

That might seem a strange word given their batting averages but with either of them you never know if a length ball is going to be blocked or hit past point or flicked past square. That is the essence of live sport, the thrill of not knowing what is coming next. We now have three fabulous stars of that blockbuster.

Ah, and yes, the Vinoo Mankad thing. A part of me says we should be scandalized. Another says, hang on, how many young scientists today know of the phenomenal legacy of Vikram Sarabhai, how many in public life know of Sarvepalli Radhakrishnan, what does Mehboob Khan mean to our twenty-something directors? Life moves on. We cannot force those that follow to remember us.

GRIT TO GREAT

17 March 2006

Playing a hundred Test matches used to be a bit like climbing Everest. It probably still is. More and more people are doing it these days but it remains the pinnacle to be on; a confirmation of longevity, for that is what performers crave for.

Longevity tells you much. It tells you about class and discipline, it means you have seen almost everything that life can throw at you and that you are still standing. It means you can play the delicate shots and the booming drives but it also means you can hang in there; go through periods without scoring runs, for not giving away your wicket is the summit to be climbed for the day. It means you can weather form and critics, both of whom can be fickle or vicious on their day, and live to tell the tale.

Playing a hundred Tests requires less time these days. Ten years ago only sixteen players had got that far, there have been twenty since. And there are five others poised to join Rahul Dravid on that list. They are all special players,

---

The Mumbai Test against England in 2006 was Rahul Dravid's 100th Test.

as Dravid is a special player. Only two batsmen on that list average less than 40. And only three more than 55, two of whom will play for India at the Wankhede Stadium on Saturday. And nobody on that list averages more than Rahul Dravid. It is a staggering achievement for a lovely young man.

Almost ten years ago he walked out to bat for India for the first time and, while we weren't quite sure of how well he could bat, he struck us as being thoughtful and intense. At times he seemed to be brooding, his eyes narrow, his smile a hundred miles away, and we wondered if it might all get too much for him. But he wanted to learn, you could see that very early, and he seemed to pack a lot of resolve and common sense into his body. And sometimes they can produce more runs for you than a cricket bat can.

And so Rahul Dravid learned to straddle two worlds. He is the modern cricketer, aware of the need for fitness and nutrition and to hit the odd ball over long on in the one-day game. And yet he is the traditional, old-fashioned cricketer, willing to respect the bowler, willing to lock horns with him, nudging a single when the boundaries seemed to be occupied elsewhere. Unlike most of his contemporaries he could have gone out to bat in the sixties and seventies and not looked out of place.

The ability to be patient is rare and praiseworthy for it means a player is willing to let a moment pass, aware that he can own the next. Insecure performers are desperate to seize the first one, they seek relief too early, their vision is small or they are nervous.

Dravid can block the first ball and the second and the third and wait for the twenty-second. It is the sign of a confident man. Steve Waugh, he once said, gave grit a good name. He isn't doing a bad job himself.

Indeed this has been a week to celebrate grit and

perseverance for few people with those qualities have disappointed others. Anil Kumble took 500 wickets and nothing better could have happened to Indian cricket. Now Dravid walks out to play a Test for the one hundredth time and we must salute appropriately; not with a whistle and a dance step but by rising from our seats and putting our hands together.

JUDGE TENDULKAR BY TODAY'S STANDARDS

3 August 2007

During a break at Wimbledon this year, Martina Navratilova said something very interesting about champion players. 'It's not about how good they are when they are playing well, it's about how good they are when they aren't playing well.' It is a statement that is staggeringly true because not everyone can play well at all times in a career.

Most good players look excellent when they are playing well and ordinary when not. The truly great always seem to have something to offer even when their game has dropped a couple of notches. That is just one reason why it has been fascinating to watch Sachin Tendulkar at Nottingham. We have condemned Tendulkar to beauty and greatness. That is a heavy burden to carry and he has done it with some style over many years. But neither Jordan nor McEnroe nor Woods have been able to look unbeatable all the time. And Tendulkar cannot look

In the Nottingham Test against England, Tendulkar scored a well-crafted 91. India won the match.

unbeatable any more unless he wills the clock back. Nobody we know has been able to do that.

But unlike a Borg, Tendulkar is looking mortality in the eye and is willing to scrap. And so if we are willing to judge him differently, we will still be able to savour his skill and let the heart skip a beat. We need to judge him as he is today, as indeed we must Ganguly, and not by the near insurmountable standards he achieved at his peak. The problem is with us for we worshipped him like a god and now condemn him for not living up to godliness!

And so if we are willing to look upon Tendulkar as a character actor, as a piece in an ensemble, we will look back with much joy at his 91 at Nottingham. Remember there are young men trying to knock his head off and he is fighting an equal battle. It was a good tough innings and it contributed to an Indian win. So too with Anil Kumble whose character shines every time he steps onto the field for India. His batting has declined alarmingly but not his grit; and his 30 runs, chiselled out with no fanfare, were invaluable. And he continues to take wickets.

Tendulkar and Kumble represent the admirable face of sport, often in short supply these days. I would like to believe that to be on the field, in the dressing room, in the team bus, at dinner with them would be priceless education for some others in this side. Sadly Sreesanth, a fine, gifted cricketer, but one with an eye on the camera as much as on the batsman, is letting this experience go by. Tendulkar and Kumble are willing to look less than perfect for the performance that will benefit the team. Sreesanth is showing a sad ability to concentrate on being a performer of another kind and is hurting the team and himself.

Sport has no place for those who squander ability. And I am afraid Team India should soon have no place for show ponies when at last they are looking like a team of scrappers. Sreesanth is a passionate young man who has been gifted an ability that is rare. But like some young men before him, he is showing a tendency to play to the gallery. It is the fastest way to ruin. It might help him to get off the media for a while, ignore the fringes of success and return to the main menu. I hope he realizes that in the sport he so obviously loves, it is his performance and not his antics, Johannesburg not Nottingham, that will win him respect.

And I hope the Test at Nottingham is remembered for the tough cricket on view, not for some of the puerile, childish stuff we saw. Peter Moores* wants the stump microphones turned down so we don't hear what his players say. It might just be easier not to say it! And if he heard some of the things being said, he might have worried about the intelligence of the boys playing for him. India contributed as well and I hope at the Oval we see more of the brilliant bat vs ball contests we have had at Lord's and Nottingham and rather less of the lip. In effect, more of the Zaheer Khan kind of cricket.

In all the years I have seen him play, I have never seen him bowl better.† He looked relaxed in delivery stride and there was a fine rhythm to his bowling. More than anything else, he was consistent. There's a story there for people who want to see it. Cut the frills and put in the yards and wait for the knock on the door.

---

*Coach of the England cricket team.

†Zaheer Khan would go on to be chosen as one of the Five Wisden Cricketers of the Year for 2007, for his performance on the England tour.

ANIL 600 KUMBLE: A QUIET TITAN BASKS IN THE SPLENDID, LONG EVENING OF HIS CAREER

18 January 2008

Many years ago, when the nineties had just come upon us, a young man with an unusual bowling action but no passport was picked for India. But selection can have side-effects and a passport was hastily organized and a vegetarian leg-spinner landed in Sharjah.

Three months later, he made his Test debut and could scarcely have imagined that one day the figure 601 would stand alongside his name. Being the engineering student he then was, he might well have thought it was, like the Avogadro number, one of those strange numbers that appear only in text books. It was far too many wickets to contemplate.

But he has soared since then. For in his corner stood perseverance, aggression and dignity, great human qualities

---

In the Perth Test against Australia in January 2008, Anil Kumble notched up his 600th Test wicket. He would end his career with a tally of 619 wickets.

if you are searching for a role model, terrible friends, it seems, if you have to become an advertising personality. There has to be something wrong there. Every time a challenge presented itself, Kumble bit his lip, locked those piercing eyes on his target and returned to the top of his run-up.

Every time the captain looked at him he wanted the ball, every time people said he didn't turn the ball he took more wickets. That is how six hundred came about. With grit and toil and a spirit that said it could be done. You can tell I'm a fan. And I'm proud to be one. I looked at a star, not a meteor.

Many years ago, I was asked to do a piece on him and we called it 'The Quiet Titan'. He worked for the watch company then and so the match seemed right. It still is. Without doubt he is the best slow bowler India has produced; home and away, on a good pitch and bad. Even the best spinners normally start tailing off, their wiles recognized, their guile no longer as enticing, their tricks a bit tired. Kumble, at thirty-seven, is amazingly picking up wickets with the same frequency, he is adding new deliveries to his repertoire and is disturbingly ahead of anyone in India as a bowler at the moment.

He is a titan and he is still quiet and thank God for that. And he is a substantial man. If he doesn't feature very prominently in the Republic Day honours list, he may not feel bad but India should.

And yet he has been the forgotten spinner. While Warne and Murali fought epic duels in print and in words, sparked debates across continents, Kumble did what he knows best. He kept picking wickets. Unlike Murali, there is no sleight of hand, not a murmur about his action. Unlike Warne, there is no scandal and he certainly won't be signing up to play poker. Each of the three enriched the sport they played and you might say Kumble was the most prosaic of all. You might say he is the bricklayer and that will do him no discredit, for this is a mighty fine structure he has built.

And as he basks in the evening of his career, not a short winter twilight but a splendid, long summer evening, he finds himself captain of India. Various people who marvelled at his insights and determination wondered why he wasn't captain earlier. That too has now come about through a strange, unpredictable configuration of events. But it hasn't taken him by surprise, for he brings to his role the same dignity and perseverance that he brought, and still does, to his bowling. Or, for that matter, to his batting. As fires raged around our game in Sydney last week, I felt comforted to know that Indian cricket was in safe hands.

I don't know how far he will go. I don't think he does either. Sometime ago, he told me that 600 would be nice but knowing him, even his targets would be dynamic, changing to accommodate changing situations.

He says he is taking life match by match and certainly no further than a series at a time but he won't be surprised if 650 comes about.

For he has got a second wind and it is blowing him towards greater success. His desire hasn't dulled, his will remains strong, the fingers are doing fine, the mind is ready for battle and there is even need to put in an extra bat into the kit bag.

Six hundred is special and it is a special man who holds that honour.

SHY AND MIGHTY: AT THIRTY-NINE, THERE'S STILL NO STOPPING SANATH

4 July 2008

Sanath Jayasuriya is thirty-nine and not yet doing all those things that cricketers look down upon while playing. He is not putting on a tie and selling real estate, searching for coaching assignments, walking into commentary boxes or indeed playing county cricket.

It's funny how your view of the world changes once you stop playing. But Jayasuriya hasn't stopped playing even though there are some in his country who believe he should. Instead, he is still taking attacks apart and thrilling his legion of admirers. One of them is writing this article.

He must enjoy it. That must seem a strange statement because surely everyone enjoys playing cricket. Not quite true. Often time dulls the instinct, selectors and administrators take the fun away, children tug at the heart, training becomes a chore, injuries seem to hurt a bit more and muscles take longer to recover. It is a battle most

---

Sanath Jayasuriya retired from Test cricket in 2008 but continues to play one-day cricket and Twenty20s. He is the second-highest run scorer in ODIs, after Sachin Tendulkar.

people lose by the time they are thirty-nine. And while Jayasuriya has had a few arrows aimed at him, he is still up and around, taking on young kids, sometimes closer to half his age. Yes, he must enjoy it.

I watched him closely this year when he turned up to play for the Mumbai Indians.* There was still the twinkle in the eye, still the excitement of a challenge before him, the satisfaction of an innings thrillingly played; youngsters are still bowling short and wide and fetching the ball from the point boundary, they are still feeding the pick-up shot that makes boundaries seem much smaller than they are. He hit a couple on the roof of the Wankhede this year and whether he plays in the IPL or for Sri Lanka, his is the wicket that is still the most sought.

Maybe that is why he is still playing, maybe there is another peak to be conquered, maybe a point to be proved, maybe just the fear of it being all over one day. But his body is holding up to the challenge, he is still turning quickly for the second and charging from point. That is the key. When the body starts complaining, it isn't fun any more.

Only twice in recent times have I wondered at the wisdom of his continuing. In Australia he seemed to be a fraction late against Brett Lee and in the IPL, young Ishant Sharma had him bowled playing late. Against the quickest maybe the eye is a touch slow in sending signals to the brain. But those are occasional moments. In Mumbai this year the crowds wanted him to go on. 'Suryaaaaaa, Surya' they chanted and he blushed shyly in the dressing room as he often does. There is little sign of the arrogance that can sometimes visit those that achieve much.

---

*In the Indian Premier League. Jayasuriya also played for Mumbai Indians in IPL 2.

But for some reason he is putting catches down. Not the tough ones that fly by, and which he could catch, but the slow, loopy ones that he would hold ten times out of ten. Could it be the eye? Surely it couldn't because balls are still being dispatched over point and through cover. But it is something worth pondering over.

I asked Marvan Atapattu, who was with us in our studio for the Asia Cup, how it was being non-striker when Jayasuriya was in full flow. Did he make it easier for he almost scored enough for two? Surely his partner didn't need to worry about things like strike rates etc.? Atapattu had a different point of view. He thought the pressure was on him to keep taking singles all the time since Jayasuriya was the player everyone, including him, wanted to watch. Sometimes, he said, you could almost try too hard to get a single.

So how much longer? Jayasuriya will be aware that he will be under closer scrutiny than most for the first sign of a lean patch will be interpreted as a sign of the end. But since he doesn't have to worry about playing Test cricket, he has longer to recover, more time to work on fitness and to get the hunger back. Sometimes, when you play every day, you don't have time to reflect on how much you really enjoy what you are doing.

Will he celebrate his fortieth on the field? I suspect he would put his money on it!

SO LONG, MR COURAGE, DIGNITY, INTEGRITY

3 November 2008

Anil Kumble and his trusted, worn-out India cap—on another head it might have been just another cap—finally walked out for the last time at his favourite Kotla. They could no longer disregard the plaintive cries from his body. In recent times it had complained of wear and tear but was happily subservient to his heart. And so he played through unbearable pain, jabbing himself all over, but not letting a soul know, as he strove towards one final ambition: winning another series against Australia.*

The announcement itself was typical of the man: no grandstanding, no ostentation, no farewell tour. Anything else would have jarred, it wouldn't have been Kumble. One of the greatest team men the game has known did his job and said goodbye. In his last Test match, he had eleven stitches and was under general anesthesia for half a day.

Anil Kumble played his last Test for India against Australia in Delhi. He retired from the game as captain of the Indian team.

*India would go on to win the series.

When the numbness vanished, when the body was overruled once more, he returned to take three more wickets.

He has timed his exit well. He wasn't hurrying batsmen the same way and the rocket ball, the fast top-spinner that has fooled many, was a rare sighting. It was inevitable. The mind schemes and plans every ball, but the body bowls it. It was taking too much out of him. And so in later years he developed the slow, loopy googly, put more fizz into the leg break and kept coming at the batsmen. He never shirked. That is why batsmen respected him and captains wanted him.

Bowling with a fractured jaw in Antigua was the most visible expression of his commitment. But it wasn't unexpected. Sourav Ganguly once said that if the opposition was 250 for 1 and he was looking around the field, there was one man who was looking straight back at him because he wanted the ball. And Shane Warne said Anil Kumble became the best cricketer he could be. He was right. Kumble extracted from himself more than what he did from pitches. And he did that because of the power of his desire.

He wanted wickets and to get wickets he had to bowl enough and to be able to bowl enough he had to be the best he could be. Every day, every ball. He didn't rip the ball as much as others, didn't turn it enough, but people didn't understand for a long time, until he went past Kapil Dev's record, that he didn't need to. He changed the perception of spin bowling, suggesting a variation from the established pillars of guile, spin and turn. He varied pace and bounce instead and did just enough with the ball to draw edges. Inevitably they would carry to slip where another giant of Indian cricket, Rahul Dravid, was waiting to catch them.

Kumble's association with the Kotla, where he bowled

better than anywhere else, was strange. The ground had a reputation for being shabby and disorganized, full of opportunistic grabbers of complimentary tickets, people whose photographs outdid their deeds. It was so unlike everything that Kumble stood for. Yet it was here that he returned to international cricket with thirteen wickets in an Irani Trophy match in 1992 and memorably took all ten against Pakistan in 1999. They will do well to remember him fondly here.

In course of time, like with the legends, we will remember Kumble by his numbers. They are extraordinary, but the picture they paint is beautiful and incomplete. They will not tell you of the dignity with which he played the game, of the integrity he stood for and of the extraordinary respect he carried in the cricketing world; as a bowler but even more so, as a man.

And now a pillar has gone. But these are cricketing pillars, not structural ones, for new pillars will emerge. And Kumble will gradually stand aside, a colossal figure looking benignly on as another takes hesitant steps towards cricketing glory. He will not be short of advice as he had for Harbhajan when with his arm in a sling he attended every day of India's training camp before the 2001 series against Australia.* Even the volatile Harbhajan talks softly and respectfully about Kumble's contribution.

I have been an open and unabashed fan of Kumble's and consider myself privileged to have seen this journey from a quiet young man to a quiet giant. At all times he has been tough and relentless, but he has also been dignified.

---

*Harbhajan Singh would prove to be virtually unplayable in that series and would play a major part in scripting India's historic series win against the Australians.

As he wiped a tear yesterday, maybe the first tear on a cricket ground, I felt another welling up in a bedroom in another city. A great competitor, a great cricketer and a great man. And a proud Indian.

FAREWELL TO INDIA'S GREATEST WAR-TIME GENERAL

11 November 2008

The sunset was warm and glowing. Sourav Ganguly chose a good day to be his last as an international cricketer. It didn't seem for a while that he had the choice but, like he has so often done, he created the opportunity and, having done so, didn't let go. And so a fine batsman has gone when still good, when still scoring runs.

Many epitaphs have been written. Sport can be fulfilling and yet cruel for epitaphs are written about men in their mid-thirties. Not surprisingly, Ganguly the captain has received as much space as Ganguly the man who competed with God through the off side.* In a sense that was inevitable for despite several fine moments with the bat, especially in one-day cricket where he was one of the greats, his legacy as captain is greater.

Sourav Ganguly retired from international cricket at the end of the India–Australia series, which ended with the Nagpur Test which India won.

*Rahul Dravid famously said, 'On the off side, first there's God, and then there's Sourav Ganguly.'

For those who value the here and now, and for those who had not yet converted to this game eight years ago, Indian cricket was in much strife in 2000. Some people had stopped trusting the outcome of cricket matches, Tendulkar had pulled out of the captaincy, India had been demolished in Australia and vanquished by South Africa at home. Somebody needed to grab public imagination, and draw back the believers in exile. It was in such times that Sourav Ganguly became captain of India. In the next four years Indian cricket grew strong and proud but, more importantly, renewed its bonds with the faithful who make it what it is. Many great innings were played in that period, fine spells were bowled, but the buck stopped at the leader. Ganguly was an excellent war-time general.

Along the way some matches were lost and many were won. But nothing quite defined Ganguly's reign as much as that moment on the Lord's balcony.* He claims to be embarrassed by it and that is a strange admission. It was spontaneous and representative of a new generation. Young men watching it said 'yes!' not because it was the thing to do but because they were part of a generation that had the confidence to give as good as they got. The bare-chested Ganguly on the balcony at Lord's became a symbol, maybe like *Lagaan* did. It was also, come to think of it, what Ganguly was all about: not rude and disrespectful but defiant and increasingly confident.

Somewhere along the way, though, an impression was sought to be created that Ganguly was more instinctive

---

*On India winning the NatWest trophy final against England in 2002, Sourav Ganguly took off his shirt and twirled it in the air in the hallowed Lord's pavilion, a gesture apparently in response to Andrew Flintoff who had done the same when England won at Mumbai a few months ago.

than cerebral, that he just did and didn't think. The instinct of a fool counts for little and it is only a qualified man that can back a hunch. In most cases instinct is derived from study anyway. But even that impression was flawed as I discovered when he accepted my invitation to do a business show on CNBC. Ganguly was on the show along with B. Muthuraman, the head of Tata Steel, and he spoke beautifully about leadership, about separating his role as a batsman from that of a captain, about how to inspire confidence in youngsters and about mistakes that leaders can make.

'The best captains get it right seven times out of ten,' he said. 'I think I get it right five times out of ten. But I know, even when I get it wrong, that my team believes I was right in trying to be right.' This was in 2004 when he was probably the best man to have led India onto a cricket ground, certainly in the years since I started watching seriously. That is about as far as a leader can go, when a team grants a leader his mistakes because it believes they were committed in the desire to be right.

It is tempting to argue that Ganguly should have played longer. But just as nobody knows when the stock markets will peak and when they will hit a bottom, so too it is with people. The highs often attain that status later and things are rarely as bad as they seem while they are happening. Who knows what the future would have held for Ganguly, for his life has rarely been predictable.

He has chosen a good moment; one that in days to come we will remember with warmth rather than sadness.

SOLID. ROBUST. FOCUSED.

13 November 2009

Sachin Tendulkar may have inspired others to write poetry, but he batted in robust prose. Not for him the tenderness and fragility of the poet, the excitement of a leaf fluttering in a gentle breeze. No. Tendulkar is about a plantation standing up to the typhoon, the skyscraper that stands tall, the cannon that booms. Solid. Robust. Focused. The last word is the key. He loves the game deeply but without the eccentricities of the romantic. There is a match to be won at all times!

But Tendulkar too was a sapling once. And his brother Ajit sheltered him from the gale, kept him focused. Sachin looked after his cricket; Ajit looked after Sachin. Twenty-two years ago, I was asked by Sportsworld to do an article on this extraordinary schoolboy. It wasn't Sachin I had to speak to, it was Ajit. When the time for the interview came, at Shivaji Park at Ramakant Achrekar's net, Ajit was there with a cyclostyled copy of Sachin's scores. And Achrekar admonished me for spoiling his child, for fear that Sachin would get distracted.

Harsha Bhogle did his first interview with Sachin Tendulkar in 1987, before Tendulkar started playing first-class cricket.

The interview was done, Sachin was neither overwhelmed nor garrulous—indeed he was so limited with his words that you had to hold on to every one of them. The piece was sent to Sportsworld in Calcutta by courier (or was it just put into a normal post box?) and then came a request for two photographs. Again, it was Ajit who produced two. When I got the cheque, I noticed they had paid me an extra hundred rupees for the photographs. They weren't mine, but Sportsworld had a policy of paying for them, and so I wrote out a cheque to Ajit for Rs 100! It was acknowledged and accepted gratefully. We lived in different times then!

It was also my first realization that young men in the public eye needed to be sheltered so they could focus on playing cricket; that they needed an elder brother, or an equivalent, to put a gentle hand on the shoulder and, occasionally, lay one the backside. A lot of other young men today see Tendulkar's runs, eye his wealth, but their brattishness comes in the way of noticing his work ethic. For Tendulkar's life is not the story of extraordinary ability but of an extraordinary work ethic.

Twelve years later, on a cold evening in Bristol, preparing for a World Cup game against Kenya the next day, I saw him in dark glasses fiddling around with his kit. Aimlessly, like he was searching for something to do. At most times he would be bounding around with energy, bowling off eighteen yards, taking catches, shouting thoughts to other batsmen. I approached him hesitantly, I couldn't see his eyes because they were shrouded by these huge dark glasses, probably the only time they were used to cover rather than adorn, for he had just lost his father. I asked him if he would talk to us about coming back to play. He nodded his head and only briefly took those glasses off. His eyes were red and swollen; you could see he had been crying copiously. For the interview, he put them on, and once the camera had stopped rolling, admitted he didn't want to return, that his mind was all over the place, that he felt anchorless. It was the only time he didn't want to play for India, but he had been forced back by his family, aware that only cricket could help him overcome his grief. When he got a hundred the next day and looked heavenwards, some other eyes were moist. Even in his grief, there was resolve, for he wanted that century. It might only have been Kenya but he was battling himself, not the bowlers.

Four years later, he agreed to do an interview for a series of programmes I was then doing. Our producer thought we would make it special and, to our surprise, and joy, Amitabh Bachchan agreed to introduce the programme. In the first break, Sachin whispered, 'That was a beautiful surprise.' Little did he know there was more to come. Sometime earlier he had told me he was a great fan of Mark Knopfler's and we thought it would be great if we could get the great Dire Straits man to talk to us. 'I'm recording all night, but immediately after that, before I fall asleep,' he said, and somehow we persuaded Sachin to do the programme in the afternoon rather than the morning! And when the moment came, we patched the line on, and when I said, 'Hello Mark', Sachin looked puzzled. A minute later his eyes lit up when he realized which Mark we had on the line. And then he was like a child, tongue-tied, fidgety, excited, much like most people are when they first meet him! Even the stars can get starry-eyed!

There have been moments of surprising candour. When asked, as batsmen tend to be, which bowlers had troubled him the most, he smiled an almost embarrassed smile and said, 'You won't believe this.' When probed he said, 'Pedro Collins and Hansie Cronje!' 'In fact,' he said, 'I once told my partner, "Will you please take Hansie for me, I don't mind playing Allan Donald"!'

Tendulkar's batting has been much chronicled over the years; indeed I believe he has been the most analysed cricketer in the history of the game. Yet, he has found the urge, and indeed the solutions, to play on for twenty years. Now that is a landmark to be celebrated, not the many inconsequential others that we exploit for our own need. It has been fantastic having a ringside view of this journey, watching a cricketer, and a person, grow. But one thing hasn't changed. He still approaches every game like a child would a bar of chocolate: feeling happy and fortunate.

TWENTY-TWO YEARS LATER

15 November 2009

All of Bombay's maidans are a stage where every cricketer has a role to play. And his seems to be the blockbuster. Ever since he unveiled Act One early last year, audiences have been waiting, a little too eagerly at times, to watch the next scene. Sachin Tendulkar is only, so far, acting in a high-school production. Yet critics have gone to town. And rave reviews have not stopped coming in.

I guess it can only happen in Bombay that a schoolboy cricketer sometimes becomes the talk of the town. Why, at the end of every day's play in the final of Bombay's Harris Shield (for Under-17s), everybody wanted to know how many he had made. For he does bat three days sometimes! And for all the publicity he has received, Sachin Tendulkar is really still a kid. He only turned fifteen on 24 April. And he is very shy, opening out only after you have coaxed him for some time. As his coach Mr Achrekar says, '*Aata thoda bolaila laglai.*' (He's started talking a bit now.) And it's then that you realize that his voice has not yet cracked.

This is the text of Harsha Bhogle's 1987 article on Sachin Tendulkar, with a postscript.

172

The beginning of the 1987–88 season saw Sachin at the Ranji nets. Once again the top players were away playing Tests and perhaps the Bombay selectors felt it wouldn't be a bad idea to give Sachin first-hand experience of a higher category of cricket. He was named in the fourteen for the first couple of games, and manager Sandeep Patil kept sending him out whenever possible—for a glass of water or a change of gloves. All along Sachin probably knew that he was still at best a curiosity, and that, while Bombay was giving him every blooding opportunity, he had to prove himself on the maidans.

And that is exactly what he did. Season 1987–88 was a purple patch that never ended. Playing in the Vijay Merchant tournament, he scored 130 and 107, and then at the Inter-Zonal stage he made 117 against the champions, East Zone. Then in the Vijay Hazare tournament (for Under-17s) he scored 175 for West Zone against champions East Zone.

Then came the avalanche. A 178* in the Giles Shield and a sequence in the Harris Shield of 21*, 125, 207*, 329* and 346*! A small matter of 1028 runs in five innings! And in the course of that innings of 329* he set the much talked-about record of 664 for the third wicket with Vinod Kambli, who, it is not always realized, scored 348*. Perhaps the most fascinating of them all was the innings of 346*. Coming immediately, as it did, in the shadow of the world record, a lot of people were curious to see him bat. Sachin ended the first day on 122, batted through the second to finish with 286, and when the innings closed around lunch on the third day, he was 346*. And then came back to bowl the first ball. In Bombay's April summer.

*

Quite often, Sachin is playing all day; important because it has helped him build the stamina to play long innings. 'I don't get tired,' he says, referring to them. 'If you practise every day, you get used to it.'

And what about that world-record innings? 'I could bat very freely then because my partner Vinod Kambli was batting so well that I knew that even if I failed, he would get enough runs for the side.'

Isn't there a lot of pressure on him now? Everyone assumes he will get a big score? 'Only in the beginning. Till I get set. Once I get set, I don't think of anything.'

Wasn't he thrilled at being invited to the Ranji nets? 'Definitely. After playing there I got a lot of confidence.'

*

The question that arises then, given all the publicity is: Just how good is Sachin Tendulkar?

'For his age, unbelievable,' says Sharad Kotnis, Bombay's veteran cricket watcher. 'He is definitely comparable to Ashok Mankad, who had a similar run many years ago . . .'

Luckily for Sachin, there is a calming influence over him, just so he doesn't get carried away by this acclaim. His coach Achrekar knows exactly what he is talking about. 'He is not perfect yet. Far from it. In fact, I would say he is not even halfway there. He still has a lot of faults, particularly while driving through the on, which is an indicator of a class batsman. He still has a long way to go . . . I don't think we should get carried away by his scores. After all, one has to take into account the nature of the wicket and the quality of the bowlers. By his standards the quality of the bowling he faced was not good enough . . .

. . . Achrekar, in fact, is quite upset about the publicity Sachin is getting. 'People don't realize that he is just fifteen.

They keep calling him for some felicitation or the other. The other day he was asked to inaugurate a children's library. This is ridiculous. These things are bound to go to his head. He will start thinking he has achieved everything. I hope all this stops so he can concentrate and work hard.'

*

Clearly the curtain call is still a long way off for Sachin Tendulkar. He has a lot of things going for him. Most importantly, he is in Bombay, where the sheer atmosphere can propel him ahead. In how many cities would a fifteen-year-old be presented with a Gunn and Moore by the Indian captain? And in which other city would the world's highest run-getter write to a fifteen-year-old asking him not to get disheartened at not getting the Best Junior Cricketer award?

Sunil Gavaskar wrote to Tendulkar to tell him that several years earlier another youngster too had not got the award and that he didn't do too badly in Test cricket. For Sachin the letter from his hero is a prized possession. Another great moment was a meeting with him where '. . . he told me that I should forget the past every time I go to bat. I should always remember that I have to score runs each time.'

He is in the right company. And the right environment. The next few years will show whether he has in him the mental toughness to overcome the overexposure. If it does not go to his head, surely there is a great future beckoning. This is really just the beginning and I will be watching this little star with avid interest for the next three years.

If he is still charting blockbusters, I'd love to do another review then.

*

India opener Virender Sehwag:

> I modelled myself on Tendulkar after watching him bat in the 1992 World Cup in Australia. I'd try to copy his backfoot punch and his straight drive, I'd copy his stance, playing the shots in front of the television as I watched him do in the match. The reason I started playing cricket was that I wanted to be another Tendulkar. Had it not been for him, I would not have ventured onto a cricket field. A lot of people have said that I bat like Sachin, but the truth is, however hard I try, I'm not even half the batsman Sachin is.
>
> Incidentally, I scored my first century in international cricket—my 69-ball hundred—using Sachin's bat. He had given his bat to Sameer Dighe, and I took it from him when I went out to open the innings. I haven't returned it.

SEHWAG–GAMBHIR CAN BE INDIA'S GREATEST PAIR

27 November 2009

Virender Sehwag thinks Gautam Gambhir is the best Indian opener since Sunil Gavaskar. He's wrong, but in a rather pleasant kind of way because it is not the subject of the statement but its maker who is the current holder of that honour. Sadly, it is not a particularly long list of players who qualify and, really, only Navjot Sidhu and Ravi Shastri can lay claim to the title. Both endured good patches and bad and so a fair assessment should only come after Gambhir has played about fifty matches. If he continues in the form he is in, or even in relative proximity to it, he should prove Sehwag right. But between them, they should be disappointed if they don't emerge as India's finest opening pair ever. The current incumbents are Gavaskar and Chetan Chauhan, a terrific combination, but these two should bat together for much longer.

Gambhir is in the form of his life, 27 Tests having produced 8 centuries. It's the kind of start Andrew Strauss

---

Gautam Gambhir scored centuries in the Ahmedabad and Kanpur Tests against Sri Lanka in November 2009.

had and indeed, for someone who goes through form swings, Strauss has an extraordinary conversion rate of a century every 3.7 Tests (which is identical to Sachin Tendulkar's conversion)! Gambhir currently scores a century every 3.4 Tests and averages almost 57. But it is in the last sixteen months really that his career has taken off. In twenty-five innings, he has 7 centuries and 7 half-centuries for an average of 77, and, just as strikingly, has only one single-digit score in it! Followers of Test cricket, they are still a pretty substantial number, will rub their hands in glee at figures like those.

And yet Gambhir is not one steeped in orthodoxy or, indeed, limited by the format he currently excels in. An outstanding CB series campaign in Australia last year marked him out as someone special, and I have little doubt that if there were to be an IPL auction today, he would be on top of everybody's shortlist. To that extent he is like the good old music director in the movies, not quite the classicist but equally at home with the raga and the remix, the folk song and the peppy dance number. And that is where he is creating a large gap between himself and other new age cricketers like Rohit Sharma and Suresh Raina, whose infatuation with the short game is limiting their progress in other forms.

I believe, and this is open to debate, that he is one of the three finest young batsmen in world cricket, sandwiched for seniority between two South Africans, A.B. de Villiers and J.P. Duminy. De Villiers, in the middle of a pretty decent patch himself and equally good in each of the three forms, averages 44 from 52 Tests, a number that is bound to go up, and Duminy oozes enough class to suggest that he would be a safe stock to invest in even if he is only 6 Test matches old.

So what could come in the way of Gambhir? For

starters, we don't know how good he can be in Australia and South Africa in Test cricket, two places India have traditionally struggled in. Of his 27 Tests, 17 have been played in India and the rest spread between Sri Lanka, Bangladesh, Zimbabwe and New Zealand. You could say he hasn't really been tested by pace and bounce but you cannot pass an exam unless you have appeared for it! He has twelve months to prepare for that; indeed that will be the start of a really stern examination for India with a tour to South Africa, a World Cup at home, and away tours of England and Australia. He will be nudging thirty then, no longer able to slip into the 'young' category, and that patch could well determine whether he has it in him to enter the portals of the greats.

Sadly, it is unlikely his record would have progressed greatly by then because India are currently a bit allergic to playing Test cricket. When you are in the kind of form Gambhir is in, you want to play as much as possible and, with just three more Tests in the next ten months, it is a pretty meagre diet he is on. It doesn't help that India are producing the kind of pitches that can only drive people away from Test cricket. I fear, therefore, that Gambhir might well be the last major Indian player whose career could be assessed by a Test record. Now that's something to think about!

SACHIN IS MORE THAN JUST A CRICKETER

26 February 2010

Sachin Tendulkar sugar-coated the recent reality of India and gave its people something to cheer about.* It is not easy to possess the mandate to lift the spirits of such a large nation, but he has done that consistently. The comparison with Sir Donald Bradman is not restricted to his batting alone. Like the great man who brought cheer to post-war Australia, Tendulkar allowed India to momentarily forget fires, bombs, inflation and terrorist threats. It was like that with the century after England so graciously agreed to tour after 26/11. It has been like that for a long time. For better or worse cricket is more than a sport in India; Tendulkar is more than just a cricketer. Where our elected representatives callously fritter away the mandate people give them, Tendulkar has stayed true to it.

On 24 February 2010, Sachin Tendulkar scored a 147-ball 200 against South Africa at Gwalior—the highest individual ODI score ever.

*Fifteen months before this match, Mumbai was hit by the 26/11 terror attacks.

180

And Tendulkar has never forgotten why he started playing the game in the first place. The best have lofty ambitions when they begin, but soon commerce, like a tenacious worm, gnaws into them. Fame surrounds them and prevents the fresh air of reason from breaking through. They acquire sycophants, that great curse of success. Playing the game becomes a means to a seemingly superior but, in reality, a hollower end. Tendulkar has kept those demons at bay. He has made more money than anyone else, acquired greater fame than is imaginable but you could never guess that from the way he plays his cricket. He remains the servant, pursues the game with purity. Through the last decade India have been well served by like-minded giants.

Tendulkar works as hard as anybody has. Lance Armstrong once said that he wins the Tour de France not when he is cycling down the Champs-Elysées but when he is out in the mountains facing icy winds while others are cozying in their blankets for an extra hour. Two years ago Tendulkar realized that his future lay in the way his body coped, that eventually his body rather than a bowler would get him. During the first IPL, as he struggled with his groin injury, he admitted that he found continuous rehab very difficult to live with. Once fit, he was like the child again, able to do what he wanted without worrying about whether his body was an accomplice or a traitor. And so he trained harder and rested well. You could see the effect as he scampered between wickets. Tendulkar's delightful second wind is the result of what you and I have not seen: hours in the gym and in training.

As a result, Tendulkar's endgame is nowhere in sight. He is peeling off centuries like he did in his prime, the old air of predictability is still around; he is grinding his way through when needed, clobbering the ball when required.

In this extraordinary long-distance race he is running, this looks like a mid-race burst rather than like the finishing kick his age suggests it should be.

So why has no one else scored a double century in limited-overs cricket so far? Well, because it is very difficult for a start. Assuming 300 balls you should expect to get no more than 150, which means you need to bat at a strike rate of 133, you should be mentally alert because one casual shot, one moment of disrespect, could be your undoing. But, let's admit, the combination of pitches, outfields and boundary ropes has rarely tilted the balance so much in the batsman's favour. At Gwalior, the groundsman told one half of the class they were not wanted; the bowlers were the extras in a movie, seeking, at best, a talking part. The stage had been prepared for Tendulkar but he still had to deliver an unforgettable performance.

Inevitably the question will be asked: What next? I know there is only one thing he genuinely covets and that is not in his hands. In twelve months Tendulkar hopes to play his sixth and last World Cup. So far his relationship with the World Cup has been like that of a child who scurries to the rosogulla shop only to find it shut everytime. If he were a golfer seeking a Masters win or a tennis player hoping to win another Grand Slam, he could plan for it, but he doesn't hold the key to a win in a team sport. It must happen; he cannot make it happen. But what else? Frankly, I don't care.

Tendulkar's journey is about joy and purity, and a landmark is merely a comfort stop.

YUVRAJ SHOULD SEEK DADA'S HELP

11 June 2010

Yuvraj Singh's dropping is neither unexpected nor unwelcome. Like a moon he has waxed and waned throughout his career: periods of breathtaking highs and exasperating lows. It is one such low that he has encountered now. And yet, I believe, he has not merely been dropped, he has been challenged. It could be good for him.

From here, Yuvraj could take either of two paths. He could shut the door and blanket himself with self-pity; he could select those around him who will speak of injustice and subterfuge; he could get angry and walk around with a snarl; worse still, he could allow himself to look and feel wounded. Neither of those are friends, not one of them will help him stage a comeback. If anything, they could ensure that his compass points south when the promised land lies to the north. Shallow, self-seeking friends are a great scourge of Indian cricket and this is a good time for Yuvraj to assess who is in his corner.

Yuvraj Singh was dropped from the Indian ODI squad in June 2010. This piece proved to be prophetic, since Yuvraj went on to become the Man of the Series in the 2011 Cricket World Cup.

Alternatively, Yuvraj could look at recent events and believe this is the best thing that could have happened to him. Yuvraj has, these last few months, been overweight and sluggish. Maybe he has been mentally overwhelmed; maybe there are too many things occupying his mind; maybe cricket was not the most important thing in his life. That can happen. When you do something every day, you can take it for granted, let your feet recede from the extra step they need to take. His franchise was unhappy with him and his ebullience had vanished. It is a situation that is crying out for dispassionate self-assessment, solitude and introspection. The selectors have thrown him a lifeline, not both ends of the rope as my friend Navjot Sidhu likes to put it.

From here on it is not Yuvraj's skill but his attitude that will determine how much cricket he plays. Other cricketers have been at the crossroads before. Some, like Nayan Mongia, a wonderfully skilful 'keeper, never came back, others, like Virender Sehwag and Sourav Ganguly, emerged refreshed and hungry for battle. Five years ago Ganguly showed his tenacity by brushing off the cobwebs that were forming around him, and ground out a glittering comeback. Ganguly's would be a good number for Yuvraj to dial, since the former captain understood his protégé like no one else.

A short period off the field could rekindle the hunger in Yuvraj, remind him of why he started playing in the first place. In his mind he could list out his priorities and rediscover that cricket should be at the top. He could ask himself if the frills have overtaken the main course in his life. He could emerge humbler towards this most magnificent of sports that has a way of telling it as it is!

Contrary to what some believe, humility and confidence are not oil and water, they are not immiscible. Being humble doesn't mean being weak, it is merely accepting that some things need to be corrected and going out and doing that.

A rejuvenated, fit, focused Yuvraj Singh could be central to India's planning for the World Cup. When in form he has few peers in one-day cricket. But that World Cup spot cannot be handed to him on a platter. It has to be earned by playing domestic cricket, by spending hours in the middle understanding himself, by staying away from the moths that flicker around a light and go away when it is put off. Doing that will demonstrate his hunger for the game and that will determine how much longer he plays.

I look forward to Yuvraj 2.0 with anticipation. It is the person rather than the cricketer that will define him henceforth. But I won't be surprised if no. 4 is one of the first names put down for India's first game at the World Cup.

SALUTING THE MAN WITH THE BIG SMILE AND THE BIG OFF BREAK

9 July 2010

Muttiah Muralitharan has chosen a good time to go. His off breaks had become a little gentler, his shoulder a bit weary, his quiver of arrows a touch lighter.

Young upstarts had just started to take him on, where earlier the idea wouldn't have entered their minds. And, in any case, he has a world record for posterity. In his decision to retire, for some the most difficult of all, Murali's timing has been impeccable. When the aura dims it is the prelude to the end.

There is little doubt that he will go down in history as a game changer. Hitherto, people with freak actions had only illuminated the skies briefly. Inevitably they were deciphered and shown to have a limited repertoire. Sometimes, especially with the faster men, the body rebelled:

When Muttiah Muralitharan announced his retirement from Test cricket at the beginning of July 2010, he had 792 wickets from 132 matches. He picked up 8 wickets in his last Test against India at Galle later that month, bringing his career tally to the round figure of 800.

it wasn't crafted to handle an abnormal workload. But Murali kept going. It had to be more than the action, for the world's obsession with it demeans him. Skill and perseverance brought him 792 wickets. If it was the action alone, a clone would have produced at least 300 by now; there would have been kids in the streets bowling like him.

Certainly they must have tried; that they couldn't is a tribute to his uniqueness. At the heart of his huge success lay the simple big turning off break, the unfashionable stock ball that all great spinners possess. Shane Warne had the big leg break and, on days when little else worked, he kept using it skilfully. Only Anil Kumble, among the greats, did not possess the big turner, but then he redefined spin bowling with variations of pace and bounce as much as flight and turn. Like Murali, he too was unique.

Murali's off break was a phenomenon of the wrist, not the finger, as it has been with off-spinners since the game was first played. And that is why he got more fizz and turn than anyone else. It made him someone to watch out for. But to achieve success he needed more in his armoury. When the off-spinner has the straight ball, or the old-fashioned arm ball, it makes the off break more potent. Murali needed something to go with the off break, a little dash of spice. Then he unveiled his doosra, by his own admission, after much effort and practice. Batsmen who came down the wicket to him would now have to ponder over that decision. The moment they played him from the crease, they had entered his kingdom.

Until June 1996, Murali only had 81 wickets from 23 matches, just about 3.5 a game. Thereafter 711 wickets came from 109 Tests. It was like he owned the mint and could stamp his own paper. I remember him bowling in a Test match in Lucknow in 1994 and almost looking helpless as India's batsmen, led by Navjot Singh Sidhu and

Sachin Tendulkar, kept coming down the wicket to him. He took 5 wickets eventually but they cost him a lot. He was still like a car that took you to the destination but guzzled a lot of petrol. Each wicket cost him 34 runs then compared to a mind-blowing career average of 22.

Thereafter only two countries stood in his way. In India he averaged 45, and in Australia, where he recognized antagonism at every lamppost, he paid 75 runs for every wicket. But against anyone else, anywhere else, he was a champion. Much has been made of his 176 wickets against Zimbabwe and Bangladesh (surprisingly little is mentioned about Bradman vs India and South Africa in home conditions against whom he averaged 201 and 178) but even subtracting those numbers (and you don't have to), he still managed 534 from 95 Tests. By the way, his numbers against England, 112 wickets from 16 Tests, were comparable.

And so, let's stop being defensive about Murali and acknowledge that he was a once-in-a-lifetime cricketer; he did things nobody else on the planet could; he played to an extraordinary level of performance day in and day out; he did every day what most people aspired to once in a lifetime. And nobody is going to touch his record. At 5 wickets a Test, which is something even the greats struggle to reach, someone will have to play 160 Test matches. I'm afraid that era has gone.

So let's salute the man with the big eyes, the big smile and the big off break. He was a collector's item because they only made one of his kind.

SEHWAG AND GAVASKAR BATTING TOGETHER WILL BE A DREAM COME TRUE FOR EVERYONE

6 August 2010

I know it isn't possible but, what the hell, we think about it all the time! We try and match players from different generations and, while that is not just unfair but impossible to do, I have been spending a lot of time (the advantage of being on one flight too many) thinking of what it would be to watch Sunil Gavaskar and Virender Sehwag, the two Indian opening batsmen at different ends of my cricket-watching interval, bat together.

For starters, both would enjoy it. Gavaskar has always said that his bread-and-butter shot was the single and he could take it almost as a ticket to the show at the other end. And Sehwag could see the powerful cocoon Gavaskar built around himself, so single-minded was he in constructing an innings.

Interestingly, an all-time great World XI that was named in 2011, based on an open poll, had Gavaskar and Sehwag opening the innings.

189

But even more fascinating would be seeing the difference in style. Gavaskar was the classical old-school batsman, body right behind the line of the ball, bat straight as a well-constructed wall (Rahul Dravid was version 2.0). One of the great joys of watching cricket for us was to see Gavaskar up on his toes, eyes like an assassin's—never wavering from the object of attention—meeting with his bat a ball projected at his throat, letting it dribble meekly down its face, now devoid of any potency, and fall dead by his toes. Gavaskar played some of the most attractive shots you will see—the straight drive was for posterity, but neutralizing the venom of a bouncer defined him for me.

To Gavaskar, and indeed to many of his generation, the wicket was a citadel that could not be breached; it had to be protected like a family heirloom. When you were sure it was safe, you played the bold shot. But you were not encouraged to hit in the air, and if you were stumped by a yard trying to hit a six when on 99, you were probably made to stand in a corner!

But when Sehwag does it, it doesn't evoke howls of protest. Sehwag is the warrior who must conquer many lands and only then return home for a meal. If he cannot attack, if the bowler's offering is so compact that shot making is not an option, only then will he defend. There are no heirlooms any more; if you lose a Blackberry you buy another. Or if you think blue looks cool, you buy another. Occasionally in trying to spear the opponent you left a flank open and paid for it, but that was just one of the hurdles of doing a job.

And so Sehwag, such a product of this generation, must play beside the line rather than classically behind it. The feet provide support to the body but don't have a huge role to play in shot making. You let the ball draw alongside and then, with the space you now possess, you either slice it to bits or smite it to the boundary. It is an altogether more violent form of batting. If Sehwag got behind the line of the ball, like he sometimes does when it is too straight, he wouldn't have the space or the freedom to play his way.

The Gavaskar approach was maddening to a bowler. Robin Jackman once told me of how Gavaskar didn't let him see the off-stump for an entire spell. 'He made me bowl where he wanted me to bowl rather than where I wanted to bowl,' he said.

The Sehwag approach is to put fear in a bowler's mind. 'He must know when he is running in that if he bowls a bad ball, Sehwag will hit it for four,' he once said. Just as a bowler can induce a tense batsman to play a bad shot, so, too, can Sehwag force an uncertain bowler to bowl a bad ball.

With Sehwag you have fear and hope, with Gavaskar, it was like hitting your head on a rock at the sheer futility of bowling. Gavaskar would never have got stumped on 99, but he wouldn't have hit a six on 195 either! Two different styles you could not hope to see in a lifetime. But at the corresponding points in their career (79 tests each) a mere 88 runs separate them. The difference in batting average is but 0.68.

Eventually, therefore, it is about doing things as you know best—as two brilliant cricketers thirty years apart have shown.

WE HAVE NEVER GIVEN VVS THE STATURE HE DESERVES

8 October 2010

In a wonderfully charming way, the world sometimes pauses, holds back from its relentless march forward, to look at timelessness, at things that defy the situations it seeks to create: a beautiful love story, a travelogue lazily told, a ghazal, a V.V.S. Laxman innings . . .

When Laxman bats he is almost dated, sepia tends to tinge the bright, colourful, high-resolution pictures that show him batting. He doesn't steal the impossible single, doesn't come storming back for a second like his life depended on it, doesn't snarl at somebody because he has a couple of seconds and doesn't know what to do with them . . . He lets the moment breathe, gently sniffs at the serenity that inevitably surrounds him and takes his stance, his world dictated by his speed and no one else's. Like Jonathon Livingston Seagull he seems to search for a higher calm as the other seagulls scrap for anchovies around.

With over 8000 Test runs to his credit, V.V.S. Laxman is the fourth highest run-getter for India ever, after Tendulkar, Dravid and Gavaskar.

Not that the scrapping is bad, not that the stolen second run is impure—it is just not him, not his world. When he was slogging in the IPL recently, his bat speed awry, his body tilted at strange angles for stroke play, the leg moving out of line to hit over midwicket rather than coming languidly towards the ball to stroke it past cover, he looked like a cheap imitation of the original. It didn't become him. It was an artist trying to enter the world of commerce; a world that pays millions to those who don't bat like him.

And Laxman is understated, another disqualification from the world of commercial endorsements. When he uses the letter 'I' it is only because it is in the middle of the word 'win'. He loves winning, he loves contributing to a win, but he is unlikely to be nudging someone to be in the first row of the photograph. And so, while the big cheques don't always appear, something else does: respect in his dressing room and in that of the opposition, like it does with Naseeruddin Shah* while the big cheques go to Salman Khan†! But respect never goes out of fashion; it is something all performers crave, and he has it in abundance.

For a major part of his career, Laxman has batted at no. 6. It means the tail is a stone's throw away. It means the boundary riders are out for him, offering him the single to attack the rest. It means he stays not out more often—once every sixth innings almost, compared to about one in ten for Tendulkar and one in nine for Dravid. You might argue it boosts his average, but the innings rarely go as far as they might have gone. Hence, only 16 centuries. Hence too, the change in batting style; from a free-stroking player

---

*One of the most critically acclaimed actors India.

†One of Bollywood's biggest stars.

to someone who must guard his wicket and prolong the innings. No. 6 is a difficult position to bat in if you are a batsman who doesn't bowl, because your numbers rarely look as good as those who precede you.

That is why Laxman has had to walk the selection tightrope far too often for a player of his ability. That is why many believe he has been underrated. Down in Australia, they think we are daft, but we have never bestowed on him the stature we have with Tendulkar, Dravid, Ganguly and, more lately, with Sehwag. And so everytime there was a new kid on the block, the attention shifted towards Laxman. And yet in the last two years (from 1 January 2009 to be precise), he has scored a century every 4 Test matches and averages 80.

Remember, too, that Laxman doesn't play any other form of cricket at this level.* It means he has to lift his game enormously for standards of first-class cricket in India are poor and, quite simply, he wouldn't have played enough. It is an assignment that can be daunting for most, and something he will have to live with for the rest of his career. Nobody knows how long that is going to be. He might have the spine but his back is asking too many questions and his knees aren't his best friends.

Many years ago a young Jonty Rhodes was batting with the legendary, but ageing, Graeme Pollock. After Jonty had called him for one single too many, the great man called him mid-pitch and told him, 'Young man, the athletics stop now and the cricket begins!'

The athletics may have stopped for V.V.S. Laxman but the cricket continues to be magical. His place in the pantheon is assured.

---

*V.V.S. Laxman played his last ODI in 2006.

INDIA'S YOUNG GUNS PROVE
THEY BELONG

22 October 2010

A young trio has been sighted, riding into Indian cricket with the confidence and self-belief that would do their illustrious seniors proud. They seem to belong, a state of existence that has thwarted many, and, indeed, have revelled in the pressure and attention that is part of the job description of playing for India. They are all batsmen, a fact that says as much about the aspirations of the young as it does about the pitches and the box office in Indian cricket. Or maybe those are related entities.

Suresh Raina leads the pack as the most exciting young player in India today. He is also probably the calmest, a fact that is not unrelated to his success. Often the person off the field has a considerable bearing on the performance of the person on it, and young Raina seems grounded, eager to learn and has a wonderful habit of celebrating landmarks without seeming to be possessed by demons.

Suresh Raina and Cheteshwar Pujara made their Test debuts for India in 2010, while Virat Kohli played his first Test for India in 2011.

And, like most people of his generation, he backs himself in attack; in a 50–50 situation, he will prefer to go for it rather than wait. In the last couple of months, admittedly in conditions he thrives on, his confidence has shone through.

There is still a question mark over playing the short ball but Raina's education isn't complete yet. It is a chapter that isn't yet on the syllabus for young Indian players, for year after year cricket is played on slow pitches and against medium-pacers. Raina is playing in an era where it is possible to be successful without really mastering the ball that is aimed at your throat, but whether or not he seeks to overcome that will be a pointer to his ambition.

There is little doubt that Raina has benefited from playing in the IPL, for he has had to walk into situations that require him to take control. It is easy to malign the influence of the IPL, and indeed all of T20, on the development of young cricketers, but never underestimate the lessons it can teach in handling pressure. Raina has learnt those, as indeed has Virat Kohli, who grows more impressive by the day.

There was a time when a violent temper and the possession of an ego unbecoming of someone so tender in years served as Kohli's identity. In recent times, he has shown unmistakable signs of maturity, of becoming more versatile; happy to bat at no. 3 in a large run-chase, at home at no. 6 as a finisher in a T20 match. His temperament seems a lot more solid now, and he paces an innings really well—a sign of someone who is good at reading a situation. It is generally perceived that the IPL, and other differently named but similar tournaments, encourage sloggers. The perception is only partly correct, but it is also throwing young men into high-pressure situations and good players like Kohli are growing as a result.

However, Kohli is yet to recognize that scoring a century, or hitting the stumps from square of the wicket, is a happy occasion, not a moment to show off the range of expletives you possess. In the course of time, like with the more level-headed Raina he will treat victory with dignity, and realize that aggression is a state of mind not of body. There is little doubt that Kohli will soon play Test cricket, as indeed it is inevitable that Cheteshwar Pujara will play one-day internationals.

Pujara has but one substantial innings behind him in international cricket, but more impressive than even the runs he scored was the manner in which he assessed the situation. The scoreboard was moving, but there seemed a calmness around him. Unlike Kohli or Raina he has chosen the more traditional, some might say the harder, route to the national team. For three years he has scored runs everywhere he has gone, and that means he has played on benign and spiteful wickets, in happy times and more demanding ones. He is as ready to play international cricket as anybody that our system can throw up. And if he does well we will have a young man who reads scriptures to motivate himself!

Each of these three will benefit, not suffer from, the presence of Tendulkar, Dravid and Laxman. It will be the best finishing school they could ask for, and hopefully it will help smoothen the passing of the baton.

RULES, REGULATIONS, INFRASTRUCTURE

WHY THERE'S AN 'I' IN TEAM INDIA

27 August 2004

It would be tempting, and egotistical, to ignore Matthew Hayden's remark about players from the subcontinent being selfish. You could call it gamesmanship, and there will be a substantial element of that, but if it hurts there is probably some truth to it.

If he had said all Indian batsmen are bandits, we wouldn't have read it a second time, we would have called it whimsical, even wild, it wouldn't have hurt. This one does, and so it merits examination. Sometimes it helps to look beyond initial feelings of outrage.

It is my hypothesis that in over-populated—and therefore insecure—countries the self will always dominate. Feelings of comradeship, of surrendering the self to the wider cause, can only arise in either a highly spiritual phase or where the performer has ascended to a level of personal calm about his achievements.

Where you are in a mob, and we are in a mob, self-

This piece was written in response to a remark by Matthew Hayden made during the run-up to the India–Australia Test series in October 2004.

201

preservation will always prevail; whether it is about catching a bus, getting out of a movie hall, or getting admission to a professional college.

So too with Indian cricket, where unless you are selfish you cannot make a mark. We have twenty-seven first-class teams and it is impossible for anyone to monitor individual players. At one level lower, it is even worse. Young players learn very quickly that it is their score, and not the manner in which the runs were scored, or indeed the situation that warranted them, that counts more than anything else.

A seventeen-year-old is bound to feel tempted to stay 66 not out even if his team loses the match than try to blast a quick 35 which won't look as impressive when the selectors compare scores. If there were fewer players to look at, a selector could make his own assessment but with the numbers in India, that is often impossible. That is why I would go so far as to say that unless you are selfish you have no chance of making it in Indian cricket.

And it is not easy to change; leopards in every profession are stuck with their spots. Actors from folk theatre will remain loud even in serious cinema, batsmen growing up on bouncy tracks will instinctively play the horizontal bat shots, people from gloomy lands will look unhappy even in bright sunshine. Players from our part of the world cannot suddenly become team players when they have survived by protecting their interests fiercely. In times of crisis, you go back to your instincts.

When a team is performing, and therefore settled, and where individuals are secure, they can rise above the self and play for the cause. Indeed, playing for the cause then becomes a greater virtue and we have seen that aspect too in Indian cricket. In Australia they learn that early because there are fewer people playing the game; the difference between being in a side and not being in it is not nearly as pronounced as it is in India.

If Australia had 500 million people, let alone a billion, they would play like a nation of 500 million, they would guard the self before aspiring to enrich the team.

The way out is to have fewer teams playing at the highest level. Apart from intensifying competition, this means only the best can play and with that comfort behind them players can get noticed for putting the team first. Twenty-seven first-class teams is a recipe for selfishness and poor quality. If we can still put out a fairly good international team, imagine what you could do with only fifteen teams. Concentrated solutions are always more potent than diluted ones.

As a result we tend to applaud individual efforts even if the team has collectively been let down. The batting average is a batsman's badge of honour, the number of centuries his entry to the hall of fame. Even his advertising contracts have bonuses linked to the number of runs he has scored, not whether his team has won.

We dance alone, not in an ensemble, we pray alone, not in a community. We cannot suddenly expect young, insecure sportsmen to become team players when most of us aren't.

Small, focused groups can be different if they breathe a different air. In India's cricket team there are many who are willing to go beyond the self. Now it needs to become addictive, it needs to spread to selectors and administrators. October might be a good time to prove to Matthew Hayden that it can happen.

HOME IMPROVEMENT

18 February 2005

For years there were hypotheses based on stray observations and a deep concern for cricket in India. There were theories, opinions, a lot of us were like the philosophers, or like scientists of old to whom ideas in the mind were the drivers of thought because numbers on paper hadn't appeared yet.

Now we can rejoice because of a pathbreaking piece of research by Siddhartha Vaidyanathan, another of our highly promising young breed of cricket writers. He has looked at data from domestic cricket over the last five years and his findings are like music to the ears. I have read his article twice and each time I have felt like old scientists must have as elements were discovered where they ought to have been in the periodic table.

The statistics he throws up are scary. In November 1999, there were eight double centuries in the Ranji Trophy; that year sixty-four matches produced thirty-three scores greater than 150 and in -220 innings there were 137

This piece was written in the middle of India's domestic cricket season.

centuries. Forget diamonds, software and backoffice outsourcing, batsmen should have been our major exports.

And yet, in December 1999, India were in Australia and in the first Test in Adelaide our middle-order was V.V.S. Laxman at no. 3, followed by Dravid, Tendulkar and Ganguly. In the five years since, only one batsman, Virender Sehwag, was good enough to challenge those four. And there wasn't a single batsman in the country who could lay genuine claim to being in that middle order. So what were all those runs worth?

They were made on flat tracks, against bowlers who took the field knowing they had goofed and should have been batsmen instead and bowled balls that allowed the batsman to score freely. It was boring, it was irrelevant, it was taking Indian cricket backwards very fast.

Indicative of that is another statistic that Vaidyanathan throws up—50 per cent of matches produced no result, meaning they were played—or, to be fair, had to be played—with the sole intention of piling on runs, producing individual records and laying the ground for a category of cricketers to whom the self mattered more than the result or the team.

Typical of that was the innings Rajiv Nayyar produced for Himachal Pradesh. It lasted 1015 minutes, produced for him the most worthless record and probably drove a few people away from the game forever.

Cricket was, and largely still is, a throwback to the old monopoly-driven era in Indian industry where wealth management was more important than product development. Two key events started to make a difference. They should have happened ten years earlier if the BCCI hadn't been deaf to the sounds coming from everywhere.

The old zonal system, creaky, incestuous and irrelevant, vanished at last. And pitches were relaid in some centres. They became livelier and a new generation understood that instead of a contest between one set of batsmen and another the game really was about a contest between bat and ball.

Vaidyanathan reports that this year only 95 hundreds have come from 282 innings, half the percentage in 1999–2000. Batsmen are having to work for their runs, the ball is doing things late into the innings and, as a result, there is a value attached to the runs scored.

But the national league, still imperfect, is the best thing that has happened. Players are playing equals, the opposition is not being bullied, they are having to travel and play in different conditions; it should mean that the top run-scorers this year are tougher than in years gone by.

This is the time to test it by sending a strong 'A' side to play away games. Let us see how good Niraj Patel, Venugopal Rao, Shikhar Dhawan and the others can be.

But while the pitches become livelier, we must avoid the risk of thinking that pitches must take wickets. They can, at best, allow good players to take wickets and that is why the first round of Duleep Trophy matches has been so disappointing.

If matches are virtually over in two days, irrespective of the quality of cricketers, it has to be a bad pitch. We must avoid the risk of going the other extreme and producing wickets where ordinary seamers can win matches. Playing for Central Zone, Murali Kartik got 3 overs in the match, Kulamani Parida only 2, and neither got a bowl in the second innings. That is poor.

Now we must cut the number of teams to no more than sixteen to twenty. Getting into a first-class team must be tough. Any match that doesn't require a team identity must go, for we need to create team players. Good physios are essential and we cannot lose our competitive advantage, spin bowling, completely. And we need to do this today, not wait for a bright journalist to discover it five years later.

THE HOUSE THAT JOHN BUILT

22 April 2005

To John Wright being coach of India meant a commitment and a privilege. It was also maddening and frustrating.

He brought rigour to a job that had largely been regarded as a pastime; a grazing ground for those that had been players and couldn't any more. He worked hard, often harder than the players. During his first few months in charge there was a mutual gasp: from the players because they weren't aware that a coach could put in so much and from Wright because he had never worked with so much talent and so much fanfare around.

He felt his way around initially, drawing a blank with the administration, and soon learnt that in this part of the world he must rely on his instinct and relationships, not on a system to get things done. India's cricket administration could be well-meaning occasionally, not even that at most times, but it could never be relied upon to deliver simple things.

He couldn't find a moment's footage on Australia, for

John Wright coached the Indian cricket team from 2000 to 2005. This piece was written when he quit the job.

example, before their tour of India in 2001. It bewildered him that nobody else seemed bewildered by it!

He had to forge a working relationship with two key people, both very different from the kind of person he was. Ideally, I suspect, Wright would have liked to work with a Dravid or a Kumble or a Srinath; or even a Tendulkar or a Laxman. Like them he was an unassuming man with a very strong team ethic and liked to work with solid systems.

Indeed, he often spoke of his utter amazement that nobody ever considered that Kumble, a rock on the field and in the dressing room, could be a permanent captain for India.

Instead he had to work first with Sourav Ganguly and in course of time with Jagmohan Dalmiya—two very strong-willed people who lived life by instinct and rather preferred a dictatorial style. Luckily for him, they had one other thing in common. They felt strongly about India doing well and that is where they found common ground, not a lot of it but enough to stand together.

Luckily for Indian cricket, Wright was quite happy to be the background man, the systems man who kept things going, put forward his point of view but willing to accept that the captain eventually ran the ship. Ganguly liked that and as a result, while they had substantial disagreements on a few issues, they were able to talk it over and indeed in private Ganguly spoke very highly of Wright's role.

His major contribution, initially, was in the area of fitness.

That is, funnily, the easiest to implement but the last to be embraced in many cultures including ours, where batting comes first, bowling a distant second and fielding and fitness form specks on the horizon.

As India grew fitter, the performances became better

and for about nine months from June 2002 to March 2003, India played inspired limited-overs cricket.

Then the wheels started to come off and it must hurt Wright deeply that, in the two years since, India returned to where they were: a slow, lethargic side that depended on individuals for a win. He admitted that India needed someone else to provide the last ten per cent; sadly that must now come to be associated with Test cricket for in one-day cricket India are unbalanced and dated.

Still, Wright turned the tide for India and, I believe, has laid the ground for another solid, hands-on ideas man to take over. I suspect he would have enjoyed coaching in a more organized environment and that may well be the challenge before his successor. India's cricket goes from being inspired to insipid, from disciplined to disorganized, in the twinkling of an eye.

A coach can at best work out the systems, it is up to the players to believe in them. It is as true of John Buchanan in Australia and Duncan Fletcher in England as it is for Dav Whatmore in Bangladesh and Bob Woolmer in Pakistan.

A new coach would do well to speak to him, to use the learning curve rather than go seeking it himself. John Wright would only be happy to oblige.

Now he'll put his feet up for a while, watch his children grow, play his guitar and enjoy his beer. But, as he admitted, he will miss the adrenalin and the excitement, the privilege of living up to the expectations of India's public, the chaos and the frustration.

A MENTOR, NOT A MESSIAH

6 May 2005

Somewhere, in this relentless obsession with unearthing India's new coach, it might have slipped some minds that coaches don't win matches. Players do and they always have. Coaches might tinker or straighten their game, play a benevolent uncle or a stern elder brother, show a little window of opportunity, maybe even open a door, but they cannot win matches on their own. And so while it is important to get a good man, we cannot look upon him as a messiah.

Any cricketer who believes so is diverting his responsibility elsewhere. That is why I love John Buchanan's theory of having a coach but trying to make him redundant. Australia's players are not encouraged to come to the coach with a problem unless they have worked out their own solution.

It suggests that a player is capable of analysing his own game, his own weaknesses and has a clear path, or at least a dusty lane, towards finding an answer. His solution is

---

This piece was written while India was looking for a new cricket coach. Greg Chappell would eventually get the job.

then debated and, between coach and player, they figure out what to do.

Otherwise it is no different from a rich parent appointing an expensive tutor and believing that both his and his child's responsibility is over.

People have played without a coach before. Viv Richards didn't have one, neither did Sunil Gavaskar or Ian Botham. Even Sachin Tendulkar, in his formative years, found that his coaches were changing faster than the calendar on his wall.

They got by because they thought about their own game and found solutions within. They might have used a bouncing board but they were capable of independent thought. All good players today are as well and that is why we need to be careful in not equating the arrival of a new coach with say, an ambulance or a fire engine.

The identity of India's next captain is far more critical. We need to have a clear policy on whether Rahul Dravid is going to take India's team to more places than just Sri Lanka, whether there is a continuing role for Sourav Ganguly at the top and, indeed, what the plan for the World Cup of 2007 is.

Finding a coach is an important part of the larger plan, if there is one, but it is not the most important.

Yes, the BCCI is late but then it has always been; yes, it seems confused but that too is not new; yes, the statements emanating from different arms of its body are disappointing but we have seen that before and yes, if you poll state representatives randomly today, you will find that the September election is of greater importance than the appointment of a national coach.

In such a situation the appointment of a national coach in isolation is a bit like appointing an interior decorator to work on a flat that has a dodgy foundation. Most of the players the new India coach will work with will be so far down the road with their technique and attitude that he can do little more than fine-tune them.

The best place for a progressive coach is at the national academy and that is why I believe we need not one, but two appointments. Along with the national coach we need a head coach at the academy; someone who will double up as the Under-19 and the 'A' team coach as well and work very closely with the national selectors and the national coach.

That is the only way we can get a supply chain going where players can make a smooth transition from one level to another. So we have two coaches in charge of thirty-five players which makes it a smaller, more workable pool.

It has long been my conviction that it is the best-administered, rather than the best-coached, team that wins matches. True, administrators don't win matches, players do, but they create the systems that allow players to do well. The two best teams in world cricket at the moment are Australia and England and the team that makes the most of its potential is New Zealand. They are the three most professionally administered.

The most wasteful teams in world cricket are India and Pakistan and there are huge problems in the West Indies, in Sri Lanka and in Zimbabwe. These are also the most poorly managed cricket boards. When India and Pakstan enjoy stability at the top, they make the right choices and that leads to good performances on a cricket field.

The appointment of a coach is merely a good choice that comes out of a stable administration. In the absence of that it would be hoping for too much to expect a hero to ride in from nowhere and take Indian cricket to the top. Those messiahs exist only in the movies.

CHAPPELL'S WAY:
NO SUGAR-COATING BUT THE MAN
IS WORTH HIS SALT

23 December 2005

When two strong personalities face off it makes for riveting drama. Prithviraj Kapoor and Dilip Kumar in *Mughal-e-Azam*, Amitabh Bachchan and Rajesh Khanna in *Namak Haraam*, John McEnroe and Bjorn Borg at Wimbledon.

Cricket throws up its challenges too, rarely as simple as a booming serve and its return or a powerful dialogue matched by another. In this theatre, things move slower, moves are made and responses are measured.

So too with Sourav Ganguly and Greg Chappell.

Much has been said about Ganguly, much has been said for him. Chappell's role in this has carried a lot less emotion; Ganguly's has been dissected, Chappell merely evaluated. It's time to look at the other man in India's soap opera.

Soon after Greg Chappell's appointment as India's coach, differences between the coach and the captain became public knowledge. Sourav Ganguly was soon stripped of the captaincy and subsequently dropped from the team.

Chappell arouses strong feelings in the two Indias that coexist at the moment. In India's thriving, achievement-driven private sector they love him. The words he writes, the language he uses strike a chord in ambitious young men and their bosses who want to get the best out of them.

He would be a valued speaker, I wouldn't be surprised at all if he receives between eighty and one hundred invitations from Indian companies every year. Indeed, in one of the corporate programmes my wife and I run we used the Ganguly–Chappell story as a case study. A majority of the younger executives went along wholeheartedly with his thought process.

At the same time, a lot of the older managers, facing change and uncertainty in their own lives, sympathized with Ganguly and thought he deserved another opportunity. That is the other face of India where, as my cousin told me, *zor ka jhatka dheere se dena chahiye.** They believed that we need to respect the past and nurture those that have been successful.

It is in this bewildering nation of ours, where one half is trying to surge rapidly ahead and the other is taking more measured steps, that Chappell seeks to make an impression. The dichotomy must overwhelm him and if that means anything, he won't be the first or the last.

His experience so far poses a wider question. Should leaders working in foreign countries change their style to suit prevailing sentiment? Or would they, in doing so, negate the very reason for their appointment?

Some have managed it better than others; Sven Goran Erikkson and Duncan Fletcher have been well accepted in England, Guus Hiddink seems to manage fine. Bruce Yardley

---

*'The biggest push needs to be given gently', a take-off from a popular tag line for a soft drink.

could never get going in Sri Lanka and I cannot imagine an outsider being asked to coach France or Italy at football.

I think it is fair to say that foreigners need to respect local sentiment and often that comes with experience. When Chappell first let fly at Ganguly the head of one of India's leading multinational banks told me he would love to speak to him about running a business in India. He had seen promotions being offered and refused for fear that there would be too much work pressure!

John Wright took the other route. He started off with fresh thoughts, with a different work ethic ('breakfast in the hotel and practice at the ground, not the other way around!') but as he started to understand India better, those close to him said he became more Indian than anyone else.

The dilemma therefore is: Should you come hard at people to drive your message home, as Wright did initially and Chappell is doing now, or should you tread softly and in doing so, dilute your message? It is a narrow path and each must walk it his own way.

Knowing Chappell as a colleague in the commentary box, as a brilliant writer on the game and, through conversations, as a hard cricketer, I don't think he will ever tread softly.

That is why he will work best with confident, committed team players and with youngsters not quite set in their ways. I think he will also put what he believes is a warm hand on a shoulder but I am not quite sure those that are insecure will always look upon it that way. If Chappell were a pill, he would never come sugar-coated.

He can be cranky and inspirational, innovative and calm, all rolled into one. When we bought into him we bought into the whole package. And I think we bought well. When change comes knocking, there will always be one or two who will feel the heat. Either they adapt or they get looked over.

In this case Ganguly is having to adapt and he can if he looks at this positively. If he scores runs, he will look Chappell in the eye and I think he will discover that this divide is not as big as it seems. Chappell has fired the first shot, now Ganguly needs to load his rifle. Only if he does that can the warriors embrace.

WANTED: STRAIGHT RULES FOR BENT ARMS

10 February 2006

Some strange things happened last week. Greg Chappell thought a bowling action looked different and got a letter from the ICC for it. Muralitharan reacted to a racist taunt from a spectator and got pulled up for it. In a free society both were entitled to do what they did and the fact that they needed to be reined in suggests a degree of insecurity. But the funniest was still to come: Moin Khan thought that India's action in appealing against Inzamam was 'against the spirit of the game'.

I must confess I am a bit wary of former cricketers talking of the spirit of the game. I believe that the moment a cricketer is willing to appeal against a batsman he knows is not out, he loses all right to talk about the spirit and the culture of the game. And if he has sledged at a cricketer, made personal remarks in abusive language, then he is a threat to this so-called spirit.

The bowling action of Muttiah Muralitharan and Shoaib Akhtar, two of the most exciting bowlers in the game, have been found suspect by many; the 15-degree rule was formulated to introduce a method of fairness into the debate.

Laws are meant to be implemented. Just as Tendulkar was out even though he had previously grounded his bat before being nudged out in that forgettable incident in Kolkata in 1999, so too was Inzamam. I'm surprised too that the ICC should want to gag Chappell. All that it seems he has said is that Shoaib Akhtar's action looks different. But that is there for everybody to see.

If indeed Shoaib Akhtar chucks that is a decision for the on-field umpires and the match referee to take and they shouldn't be getting influenced by what people are saying. In any case they have been pretty active with young Johan Botha now joining Shabbir Ahmad on the banned list.

But it does raise the question of what should be allowed and what shouldn't. There were some pretty respectable names in the ICC panel that worked out the figure of 15 degrees as the acceptable limit. It was based on the principle that below that number the naked eye would not always be able to discern the straightening of the elbow. A logical inference therefore should be that anything that suggests a straightening of the elbow to the naked eye is likely to be more than 15 degrees.

Shoaib Malik was reported, so was Harbhajan, but the list of bowlers who seem to bowl with a degree of bend is much longer than that. It includes Murali and Shoaib Akhtar and, off the top of my head, Brett Lee, Mohammad Rafique, Shahid Afridi, James Kirtley, Jermaine Lawson and Kyle Mills. Some have suggested that Andrew Flintoff, when he bowls round the wicket, falls into that category as well.

However, the law seems a bit different if you have an anomaly in your physique. So Shoaib Akhtar being double-jointed at the elbow (and apparently at the shoulder) is allowed a greater leeway because of hyper-extension, meaning the elbow actually bends the other way rather than towards the shoulder as in most people.

However, he doesn't bowl with the elbow continuously bent; there is a whiplash action because of the act of straightening it. That, to my mind, is unfair because it allows him a bend of greater than 15 degrees.

What it also seems to do is to put him out of the purview of a bowling review because according to the law hyper-extension is not covered, being a unique natural phenomenon; which is what has caused the genial John Wright to ask if he could bat with three hands if he had them (and at times you need to take the law to an absurd situation to emphasize your point).

I think it is only fair that Murali and Shoaib be included in the legal process like everyone else. In all fairness Murali has got himself tested many times, voluntarily and forced, but Shoaib is a bit shy of that. I think just as Shoaib must have a fair opportunity to play cricket, a batsman must have a fair opportunity of knowing whether the ball coming at him has been legally delivered and, indeed, whether he is in physical danger as a consequence.

On ESPN I was watching a game from 1973 between England and the West Indies. Keith Boyce, whose action had mesmerized me as a young teenager, was bowling as indeed were Gary Sobers, Bernard Julien, John Snow, Geoff Arnold, Derek Underwood, Ray Illingworth and Lance Gibbs. Every single one of them bowled with an absolutely straight arm. Boyce and Gibbs, in particular, were actually beautiful to watch. If bowlers could bowl with straight arms in 1973, I wonder why they cannot in 2006!

SANATH TO SACHIN, THE BODY HAS ITS OWN STORY TO TELL

7 April 2006

Sanath Jayasuriya should have gone out of Test cricket at the Premadasa Stadium with thousands of noisy, but friendly, Sri Lankans singing 'Thank you for the cricket'. He deserved it but he didn't get it and that is the difference between our own scripts and those that life writes for us sometimes. A dislocated finger, a corner of a dressing room, a beautiful but small little town in the hills of Sri Lanka . . . not quite the last exit for one of the more influential cricketers of our time.

He has got the order of his exit timed correctly though for his style is now more suited to the one-day game, to the classic cameo rather than the lead role; a few thrusts of the rapier, the sudden burst to the other end and, very often, a more surprising burst back for a second, a quiet little squat between deliveries and then a carve over point.

He will leave Sri Lankan cricket with a hole at the top. Over the last few years, they have had two talisman

Sanath Jayasuriya retired from Test cricket in 2006 but continued to play one-day cricket till 2011.

cricketers: Muralitharan spinning the ball with a smile and Jayasuriya slashing it away with a smile. Murali's forte was Test cricket for a bowler just about gets a speaking role in one-day cricket. That was Jayasuriya territory and he was a giant, holding up the side and yet, in doing so, allowing a huge shadow to fall on it. Sri Lanka have never really emerged from that shadow and now they must. As Glenn McGrath made the other bowlers look better, so did Jayasuriya with the batsmen. Now the Sangakkaras and the Jayawardenes must walk alone.

Jayasuriya cannot do much more for the body is giving way now and the spares cannot arrive. The mind will be willing but it cannot perform alone for sport requires a combo. Often when the mind is strong it drives the body forward, like an officer might his troops. But once the body starts complaining, once the reserves start to run dry, the mind grows weary. The director knows the script but the actors cannot perform any more. And once the mind starts questioning, the end for the athlete is nigh.

Jayasuriya has taken the right decision and that is something Sachin Tendulkar must ponder over as well. It is not a verdict he needs to arrive at just yet, maybe, but it is a possibility that must enter the vast territories of his mind. Even if not the preferred one, it must enter the spectrum of options. Different parts are creaking now and like weary salesmen they want to rest in between. Invariably the body throws up other options, another muscle gets used a little more maybe, but they cannot take the workload and soon they complain too. Tendulkar's joints, his muscles, were like performers in a circus moving to the ringmaster's tune. Now they resemble partners in a coalition, they need to be kept satisfied. Maybe that is the challenge: drive the body and then rest it, and once rested, tease it and ask it, 'do you want more action?'

And so, really, the greater worry is not Tendulkar but Sehwag. Tendulkar has already produced his magnum opus and it stands there for us to admire but Sehwag's big moments still lie ahead. Maybe he can still be India's next captain but for that he must look at himself a little more carefully. Many years ago, on one of his corporate roadshows, Anil Ambani was asked by an overseas investor if he could trust him to run a company when he couldn't look after his own body. The younger Ambani shed weight like a tree might its leaves during autumn and emerged fitter and, in the eyes of the world, more responsible. So too must Sehwag for he looks a picture of neglect at the moment.

The mind is the champion but the body has its own story to tell.

STRONG BENCH ANSWER TO BURNOUT QUESTION

28 April 2006

I must confess I am completely bewildered by all the rhetoric surrounding the issue of player burnout. A simple issue between two sets of people acquires the hue and venom of a monster. There have been exhortations of a strike which leads me to believe that well-paid cricketers are actually helpless bonded labourers in disguise; that players are awakened before dawn and made to work in quarries until well after sunset.

Essentially the question of how much cricket a player should play is an issue to be sorted between those who run the game and those who play it. If there can be no meaningful debate, if a meeting point is impossible, then organizations are in deeper trouble than mere scheduling of matches. Both parties need each other and more difficult issues than these are routinely sorted out. Where trust doesn't work, commerce does.

The question of player burnout has become a topic of discussion over the past few years as a result of packed cricketing schedules that are more demanding on players than ever before.

And people adapt. I have met a lot of medical representatives who go from shop to shop, from doctor to doctor, sit long hours in chambers and travel for hours through rain and sweat. And they have to deliver every time, otherwise they lose their salary raise and bonus. And they have to perform under pressure because very often they are the sole breadwinners. And they travel twenty-five days every month, month after month, year after year. I look at them and I think nobody can do their job but they do and a lot of them do it very well. They adapt to a life of great stress because they have no option. If one existed, nobody would be a medical rep; nobody would work through night and day at Siachen. But people do. And they adapt.

The way out is not to spew venom at the ICC, not to look upon it as a cruel emperor out to torment suffering subjects, but to understand that they are merely a collection of representative bodies and cannot function in the event of a discord. If cricketers believe that too much cricket is being played, then they need to look at what their own parent body has agreed upon. And Malcolm Speed* is right when he says that the Frequent Tours Programme is a very acceptable load on cricketers. It is when cricket authorities start adding to it that the problem begins.

But let us for a minute assume that the amount of cricket a country plays goes beyond the reasonably accepted. Maybe we need to change the way we look at the squad. Maybe the way out is to look at larger squads with players coming in and out depending on their fitness levels and the need for rest. It happens all the time in football and I believe that is the way ahead in one-day cricket.

---

*CEO of the ICC.

It has other implications as well. Teams will then need to have a stronger bench to allow easy entry and exit of players and it will allow countries with greater depth to move ahead. There will then be an emphasis on building not just thirteen or fourteen quality cricketers but as many as twenty and that cannot do the game any harm. Teams that have fitter cricketers will be able to put out their best team on the field more often, those that cannot will need to seek replacements. That is fair.

It will also address the real issue behind too much cricket which is that players run the risk of merely turning up; of treating a match like just another day at work. It is natural for players, on some days, to wish they were somewhere else and on such days, someone else can take their place. I can assure you that if that happens more than a couple of times, cricketers will remain charged up.

But these are issues that the BCCI must address for it is up to them, and nobody else, to decide. But they have to draw the balance between the playing of the game and the revenue more cricket can generate. Currently they give the impression that gathering revenue is their primary priority but like players, administrators must eventually be judged not just by the profits they generate but by the quality of their cricket team. And if they can sit across the table and sort things out with cricketers, nobody will talk about burnout.

CRICKET SHOULD LOOK FOR A FEW GOOD MEN WITH NO STAKES

5 April 2007

My father had a very interesting approach to people who came to him for, for want of a better word, 'tuition'. He had two conditions. 'I will accept no money and you will come at 6 a.m.,' he used to say, and we often wondered why. Much later I realized that this was his way of ensuring his independence. By not accepting money, he was not beholden to these students, and didn't have to put up with them, and by asking them to come at 6 a.m., he ensured that only the truly committed came to study.

I remember this story for two reasons. Indian cricket needs help but first, it needs to find people who are not beholden to it and who are committed to it. When you have a financial stake in Indian cricket, your honesty can be threatened, your voice can be stifled. But if you have nothing to gain, and only integrity, pride and commitment to offer, you can speak up for what is right. The BCCI

After the World Cup debacle, Indian cricket and its administration were at a crossroads, looking for, amongst other things, a new captain and coach.

needs such people but I am not sure they are searching for them.

Instead, the BCCI waits while Indian cricket burns; it waits for this rare configuration of elements that will take place on 6 and 7 April. For the last four days Indian cricket has been lying wounded with attack after attack made on it. But there has been no attempt to douse the fires, no damage control. If ever you wanted proof that an organization cannot be run by committees, here it is. If someone finds worms in the chocolates you sell, you don't wait for five days for people to arrive from different parts of the world to decide what to do. A leader, somewhere, takes ownership of the situation. Who then, leads Indian cricket?

That is why I believe the various vice-presidents and secretaries and holders of other currently irrelevant titles have let themselves down. Not just because they did nothing, but because they fanned the fires themselves by making statements all over the place. The obsession with the media, with the thirty seconds of fame and two days of notoriety, will be the eventual ruin of Indian cricket.

And so we need a dictator, a benevolent dictator, which is really what the head of a family is. Many years ago I had suggested that Indian cricket is a 'poor little rich kid' desperately in search of parents. Little has changed to cause me to alter that opinion. The kid is hurt at the moment and has stumbled but is there someone to give it a hand, a warm embrace; is there someone to take ownership of the kid?

So then, who leads Indian cricket? Who is it whose chest puffs with pride and who says 'this is my baby'?

And until we find this benevolent dictator, all these meetings will have little value. If, on 6 April, many captains and many vice-presidents and many secretaries are going to sit around a huge table wondering what to do next, they might as well call it off now and save everyone a lot of time and money. One person has to decide where Indian cricket goes. He can seek help, advice, opinion, comment, whatever, but one person has to decide. Alex Ferguson decides for Manchester United, Ali Bacher did for South African cricket and, at a vital moment, Indira Gandhi did for India in December 1971. Fifteen people talking together in a room will mean, at best, thirty cups of tea and coffee and five packets of biscuits consumed. No more.

There are immediate issues to be decided. The coach, the captain and therefore, the future of many senior players. There are reports to be discussed and the perpetrators of leaks have to be identified and put on television as villains. And someone has to ask: Why are the nine players, including, presumably, Sachin Tendulkar and Sourav Ganguly, so worked up? What does an admirable person like Rahul Dravid have to say? And most important: even if the manner of delivery of the coach's message was unpalatable, was the message wrong?

Are we saying that the attitude of the players cannot be questioned? Were players playing to stay in the team? By taking the easy way and sacking the foreigner we cannot bury the questions he has raised for he might be right on many counts. If Chappell goes and there is no inquiry into player attitudes it means we are perpetuating the star system and creating the atmosphere for further decline in our cricket.

There are no overnight answers to these questions for the process must begin with identifying a full-time leader who will take responsibility for the situation. Then you need to appoint a captain, guarantee him freedom, look for a coach, ease tensions in the team and look for a cricket committee of no more than four or five people who have passion, integrity and humility, to meet six times a year to review where Indian cricket is going. Not to take decisions but to check whether the plan is on stream for decisions can only come from one leader.

And to prevent hasty decisions, the tour of Bangladesh in May must be rescheduled forthwith. We can issue Bangladesh guarantees, if necessary payments, but a hastily put together team at this stage can do nobody any good.

Oh, and as a postscript, when Australian cricket was faced with a similar situation in 1985, they appointed two honourable, proud men as captain and coach, decided that players would be picked on attitude and that if it meant some good players had to leave, so be it. It served them very well but remember it was backed by a desire to do good. Can Indian cricket take a similar call?

CONSTANT CHALLENGE WILL LEAD TO CONSTANT ATTITUDE

4 May 2007

'Warning: Drug Offence Punishable by Death', the signs read all over Southeast Asia. It is blunt and chilling. No inquiry, no trial, no benefit of doubt, you can't get more direct. As I wait for my flight, I can't help wondering whether a similar approach wouldn't do Indian cricket a world of good. 'Warning: Poor Attitude Punishable by Instant Omission' sounds like a good line to put up in dressing rooms all over India.

Poor attitude doesn't mean hoping your team loses or, to give it a more sinister motive, conspiring against your team. It means you are not willing to go that extra mile, extra yard sometimes; that the extra effort is not attractive enough. You meet such people everywhere and their numbers are a good indicator of the quality of the team. Teams where player attitudes fluctuate are inconsistent. India are in that boat and that is why I believe Indian cricket finds its level of equilibrium around number 5 in the world.

Poor attitude was one of the reasons cited for India's disastrous performance in the 2007 World Cup.

From time to time, situations develop that cause average teams to improve, say to number 3. It can happen. Electrons jump to another energy level, political warlords feel the need to be honest! However, since this higher level is not a comfortable, or a practical, state to be in, it is unstable. As the scientists would say, it is not in steady state and so forces appear that nudge a team back to the preferred, or comfortable, equilibrium.

Players get complacent, they start enjoying the perks of success and, in doing so, sometimes lose sight of what made them successful in the first place, the media tells them that they are far better than they actually are. Attitude suffers and the team begins its descent. Inevitably the downward momentum takes it beyond the state of equilibrium and down to, say, number 7.

Now, new forces get triggered. Criticism hurts, finances take a hit, the same media mocks at the team, pride bursts through those layers of complacence and the players acquire a mission. That is why, I suspect, India are at their best when down and at their poorest when, relatively, on top. The difference between teams that yo-yo and those that exhibit steady performance is attitude. It is the answer to all of Indian cricket's worries, on the field and in the boardroom.

It is also, like the fountain of youth and the perfect portfolio, a little difficult to find.

So how does one guarantee constant attitude? I believe constant challenge is the answer. With great players and teams, the challenge comes from within. From a desire to be better. That is why a Borg won and a Federer does, Woods and Jordan did, and this Australian team does. For the more ordinary, for the lesser inclined, it must be enforced. And the only way to do that is to ensure that the periphery is stocked with enough hungry cricketers.

The problem though is that players on the periphery are swimming in the same pool; in the same easy, unchallenging waters. So how do we make the waters deeper, how do we let a couple of sharks in? The answer is staring at us. Sometimes we search too hard and believe that the most obvious has to be a mirage, a decoy. So we look for people who have the keys to the kingdom of knowledge, we search high and low, near and afar. Or maybe we see the obvious and it is unpalatable. The search is unnecessary but convenient.

We have at least 300 players in first-class cricket. We need to knock off 170. Ah, the administration says, we are denying them opportunity. It is one of the great fallacies of democracy. The only opportunity to offer is the opportunity to play for India and if players are not good enough to make it to the top 130, they are unlikely to be good enough to make it to the top twenty. So we must be kind to these players and let them go; to pursue another career, to have a life beyond thirty-five, maybe a more fulfilling life than that of a failed first-class cricketer. By weeding them out early, we will do them a favour.

Merge the teams of Kerala with Tamil Nadu, Goa with Karnataka, Hyderabad with Andhra Pradesh, Baroda with Gujarat and Saurashtra, Punjab with Haryana. Or maybe find another route. As Gandhiji said: Have purpose, the means will follow. Competition does lovely things to minds we have assumed are unwilling or incapable. Young men and women in the knowledge industry are taking on the world, slickly made Indian cinema has begun making inroads globally. So, why not Indian cricket?

We need to move that state of equilibrium from number 5 to number 3. And the longer we dilly-dally on domestic cricket, the longer we will take to make that move. If we don't reform cricket now, today, it means we are happy with where we are.

NONE TO WITNESS A SUNSET IN INDIAN CRICKET HISTORY

6 July 2007

As we bowed in homage to Dilip Sardesai, those dancing feet now static, Nari Contractor said to me: 'Have you noticed how many current Mumbai players are here?' I wish he had never said that, for the heart was already heavy. There were none. Sardesai's generation, dwindling at an alarming rate, was very well represented, the next generation had some marked present but contemporary Mumbai cricket had either forgotten Sardesai, or didn't care, or, hopefully, were not in Mumbai.

Indeed I wished at that moment that every young Mumbai Ranji Trophy cricketer was out of the city, for I cannot imagine that people can be as immune to history as this. Or is this a vain hope? There weren't too many when another of my childhood heroes, Eknath Solkar, passed away either. So then, are we so locked in the present that

Former Test cricketer Dilip Sardesai passed away a few days after the seventy-fifth anniversary of India's first appearance in the Test arena, which went unmarked.

we have no time to look back, to fold our hands and lower our heads in gratitude?

Yes, gratitude is the word because no generation can survive in isolation. It receives the baton from another and passes it on when the time comes. And when another time, like this sad one, comes you go back to the person who passed you the baton and say 'thank you'.

One generation not only provides inspiration, and a legacy, for another; it gives birth either to confidence, or only sometimes, to despair. Until 1971, we did not believe that England could be beaten in England; until 1959, we did not believe Australia could be beaten; until 1968 nobody thought India could win a Test series overseas.

But that generation had belief instilled in it by the deeds of Mankad and Umrigar who doubtlessly were inspired by Merchant and Nayudu. It was thus that a Gavaskar arrived, his desire for excellence fuelled by the deeds of his uncle's* generation and it was thence that a Kapil Dev came.

If one set of players had not played for Rs 200 and come by local train to play international cricket, if another hadn't received Rs 10,000 per Test, yet another would never have got more.

This generation has reaped the benefit of the popularity that was sustained by many; not just the Umrigars and Hazares and Mankads and the magical spinners but even the Jaisimhas, the Durranis and the Sardesais. It was their stories that kept cricket alive in middle-class homes that, we now forget, are the real custodians of Indian cricket.

But should we be surprised? On 25 June, it was seventy-five years since the great C.K. Nayudu lead India out at Lord's. It has been an intriguing, satisfying,

*Madhav Mantri, a wicketkeeper for India.

depressing, pulsating, emotional journey. You can use a word you like but you have to admit, it has been unforgettable.

But the sun rose that day like it were any other day and set without having enriched Indian cricket. What an opportunity it was to tell the story of Indian cricket to those in their teens for they must soon become the bastion of Indian cricket.

They know of the Gavaskars and the Kapil Devs, and lately of the Kumbles and the Tendulkars. But they need to know that Polly Umrigar once played a stirring Test match in Port-of-Spain bowling 72 overs for 124 runs and 5 wickets apart from making 56 and a second innings 172 not out in a little over four hours; that Tiger Pataudi played with one eye and one leg before a disbelieving audience in Melbourne.

If Indian cricket is shy of tradition, can we blame young cricketers for giving Solkar's and Sardesai's funerals a miss? Or maybe there is a celebration planned after all? On 19 September or 17 April or 22 July or some such insignificant date? Or maybe on 25 June 2008 to mark the end of seventy-five years of India in Test cricket.

Sadly, this cannot be a joke. The time to go, to leave this stadium of life, is not a decision we take. As one generation dwindles, we lose the opportunity to honour it.

Worse, we lose the opportunity of inspiring another generation, of telling them where their roots lie, of the land their elders came from, the ground they trod on.

What a moment it would have been for a Yuvraj Singh to see Tiger Pataudi walk up a stage in pride. Or, for that matter Salim Durrani and Abid Ali and Bapu Nadkarni and Nari Contractor. And many more.

In the end, it is the respect for what came before that symbolizes a culture. Mumbai's young cricketers let themselves down by not paying respect to one of their best.

ZERO TOLERANCE: THE ONLY OPTION

28 March 2008

Like with most things about cricket, playing a fast short-pitched ball for example, everything seems easier from a distance. A lot of us who write about the game have two things in our favour: we often sit in comfortable rooms and let the mind wander and more important, we are rarely accountable for our writing. So it is with most comments about the ICC, everybody's favourite whipping boy. It is a broad-spectrum victim, anything is game for an attack. But the ICC isn't really an independent entity, it is made up of sharply polarized nations who respect it depending on how convenient it is to do so, and is only as powerful as the nations that constitute it allow it to be.

The fact that the ICC is made up of a very small number of nations makes the job more complex. I can see people within the ICC bristling at this suggestion but the truth is that for all the associate and other members, it is really made up of three or four countries with five or six

---

In 2008, the ICC took a stand by deciding to adopt a zero-tolerance approach to abusive language and behaviour on the field.

others deriving importance from who they vote for. Even those are really satellite nations merely making up the numbers, like minority parties in a coalition. If the ICC was made up of a hundred countries, life might have been easier since no one country would have counted for much. And the game would have moved on without one or two members. But things being as they are, being head of the ICC is now a bit like heading a warring joint family.

Everyone expects the ICC to find a solution to everything. They might, if they had the power to find and enforce one. As things stand, the ICC has little power on most matters and that is something for each member nation to think about. The supposed ineptitude of the ICC is really the fault of each of the countries that make it up. It is a very tenuous bond that holds it together at the moment. Everyone wants a central governing body but nobody wants it to be strong. It's like saying I want a mathematics teacher but will not accept the marks he or she gives me.

And so nobody is happy with the zero-tolerance approach to sledging. Well, I am happy to say I am. Some cricketers are saying it will take something away from the game. Of course it will. It will take away a tumour and last I knew taking away a tumour left a person in better health. A glare on a field, a passing comment, a sarcastic remark, yes, that is part of the game because frustration and disappointment are part of the game. But abuse isn't, and sadly, the people who speak in favour of sledging belittle abuse. It is all very well to say that racial and personal comments should not be allowed. It is a naïve statement because, as we saw in Australia, we can spend hours debating what is racist and what is offensive to a certain culture.

By complaining about a solution and not contributing

to an alternative one, we take the easy way out. And if no solution is acceptable, I'm afraid you have to take what you get. And the only alternative, one that cricketers have brought onto themselves, is that there will be no sledging at all. A lot of mighty fine players scored a lot of runs, took a lot of wickets and stood close in without needing to abuse anyone. And if they could do it, everyone else should. Don't forget too that we are breeding a generation that thinks calling people offensive and rude names is part of cricket. Aren't we meant to be caretakers of the game? Handing it over to the next generation in a better state than the one we received it in? Well, all those who talk of the spirit of the game need to ask themselves this.

Making offensive remarks about a person, his family, his religion or his country doesn't make the game healthier. Those that seek to justify it will leave the game poorer.

PIETERSEN'S LEFT TURN IS NOT RIGHT FOR CRICKET

30 June 2008

One of the great truths of sport, whether you have played it at international level or are a passionate spectator, is that the game is always easier from ninety yards away. This is true for two reasons. Quite apart from the fact that you don't actually have to play the ball or bowl it, your decision is not put to test. A batsman or a bowler or, particularly, the captain has to take a decision and either bear the brunt of its failure or bask in its success. Watching from ninety yards away, you can be wrong but that doesn't impact anything.

That is why I have a touch of sympathy, only a touch, for Paul Collingwood. He wanted to win, that is the reason you must play sport, and on the spur of the moment he took a decision* that he thought would help his side to

---

In a match against New Zealand, England's Kevin Pietersen made the controversial move to 'switch-hit', i.e., change his grip to become a left-hander from a right-hander after the ball was delivered. The MCC said he was within his rights to do so.

*Appealing for a run-out when a batsman had fallen after colliding with a fielder.

239

win. Upto that point, his action could be understood and I am willing to stick my neck out to say that a lot of cricketers would have done precisely the same thing. But, in a fine piece of umpiring, he was offered the option to change his mind and that is when the ability to be calm, such an integral part of leadership, should have risen to the surface. That is when he should have recalled Grant Elliott.

So, maybe we should start putting this in the rules as well; that if a player is brought down, intentionally or otherwise, and as a result of the act he cannot complete a run, the ball becomes dead; assuming of course that a catch wasn't being taken somewhere else at the same time. (I can see other implications here: What if it is the last ball with 1 to win and you bring the batsman down? This argument is more about the spirit than about the letter of the law!)

I also believe the ICC needs to take a very firm view on switch-hitting. When the MCC, the guardians of the law and the spirit of the game (and surely that has to be wrong—it has to be the ICC, not the MCC), say it is okay for Kevin Pietersen to change his grip, and effectively become a left-hander, they are letting the bowler down. And lest we forget, for we do so too often, the bowler is an equal shareholder in the game of cricket. At the heart of our game lies the contest between bat and ball and when that is imperilled, the game is imperilled.

There are rules to bowling and batting. When the bowler delivers a ball he is presenting the batsman with a challenge. The basis of this challenge, which can never change, is the line and length he has chosen and the field he has set. These are the cards he holds. The batsman now has to respond to this challenge by offering a shot. If the field is moved in the process of the ball reaching the batsman, it is unfair on him because the goalposts are being moved, the challenge is being amended, without him being aware of it. That is why it is against the spirit of the game to do it. So, just as the batsman enjoys the security of a fixed challenge, so must the bowler. If the batsman alters the foundation on which the challenge has been presented to him, he is wrong and he must be stopped.

That is why a right-handed batsman must remain a right-handed batsman. If he becomes a left-handed batsman after the ball has been delivered, he is conning the bowler and because the bowler delivers his cards first, he has no comeback. That is unfair and undermines the very foundation of cricket, which is a fair contest between bowler and batsman given identical conditions for both. Indeed, I will go so far as to say it is immoral. Admittedly, it requires an extraordinary level of skill to switch hands in such a short while and still hit the ball for six, but then extraordinary skill doesn't make things lawful. We would have to legalize pickpocketing otherwise.

To allow switch-hitting, we must allow the fielders to change positions after the ball has been bowled, allow the bowler to go over or round the wicket and to bowl right- or left-handed without informing the umpire or the batsman. This list could get longer. The easier, simpler and more honourable way is to preserve the sanctity of the challenge; the bowler sets his field and chooses his line and length, the batsman responds, and nothing changes in between.

UNEASY TRUCE GETTING WEAKER BETWEEN CRICKET'S CULTURAL BLOCKS

1 August 2008

I'm afraid however diplomatically we seek to put it, the cricket world is torn over Zimbabwe and the Champions Trophy. The Pandavas and the Kauravas stand opposite each other, Arjuna and Karna with arrows poised to strike, Duryodhana and Bhima with maces in hand. Isn't that Tybalt, sword drawn, heading towards Mercutio who mocks him? There is no blood in this fight but the Capulets and the Montagues are in their respective quarters and we know nobody is going to win.

Our little world of cricket, and it is a very very small world, has always had two distinct cultural blocks with the odd statesmen in either camp. Each block is going to look

---

The 2008 Champions Trophy, scheduled to be held in Pakistan, was postponed after several teams refused to play in Pakistan citing security risks. At the same time there was a move to remove Zimbabwe from international cricket for some time due to the sensitive political situation in the country.

at events from their cultural understanding and try as you might, you cannot change that. You can educate people, you can ask them to be accommodating of each other but inherently, people are different and will view things differently.

As I type this I have just returned from an early morning walk through the bylanes of Varanasi heading towards the Ganga. I looked at the scene through the eyes of a visitor and found the filth unbearable. And then I looked at the devotees there and they didn't seem to mind things at all. The filth didn't come in the way of their faith. So too it is with the situation in our part of the world where we have a comfort factor with events that might cause others to back away. And as we are now discovering, the uneasy truce we had, the shifting common ground, is getting weaker.

As someone who is going to work on the Champions Trophy I would dearly love to see the world's best teams at full strength. Contrary to what some others think, I quite like the Champions Trophy because it is a concentrated tournament with the world's best playing against each other in equal conditions. But I can see why no administrative body can force its players to travel to a place they feel uneasy about, even though, as someone who has lived on the subcontinent all his life, I am aware that things are often projected to be worse than they actually are.

I am afraid this stand-off is going to continue, maybe even get worse, in the violent times we live in. The two cultural blocks in world cricket exist in two completely different milieus and if anything, in an era when the world is getting flatter, and geographical boundaries are disappearing in the intellectual world, it is only going to get worse. Cricket needs to find a solution where one team does not constitute 12.5 per cent of the total. If two countries come together they represent, effectively, a quarter of the cricket-playing world! Everybody can hold everybody else to ransom!

The only option before us, and I am guilty of repeating what I have said before, is to have more teams, so that the reluctance of some teams doesn't create an emergency. We need to have fifty–sixty teams across the world, representing cities with windows put aside for international cricket. And so, the moment four teams have a problem, they can be replaced by four others. My gut feeling is that teams may not threaten to pull out if they know they're dispensable.

At the moment we are in a joint family where if two brothers out of four do not get along, it leads to a tense household. And just as the joint family system broke up leading to nuclear families the moment it became economically viable to do so, so too it will be with cricket. For let's face it, if it made economic sense, England, Australia, New Zealand and South Africa would be very happy to coexist by themselves just as India, Pakistan and Sri Lanka would. Thankfully that hasn't happened, and is unlikely to in the current way of life.

The change has to happen in the mind. That is what the internet did, that is what digital music did, that is what automation did long ago. It started with the acceptance of changing times and that is what cricket needs to do; to look beyond narrow constituencies towards a world with fewer, different boundaries. Let's move on. Our game is stronger than the petty regionalism we seek to confine it to. Let's create a world with fifty teams.

DREAM FAREWELLS CAN'T BE
SCRIPTED IN BOARDROOMS

3 October 2008

So, either there is a voluntary retirement scheme or its equivalent in Indian cricket or there isn't. Either way, somebody is looking stupid.

If indeed there is one, it is time to mourn, for it undermines a cricketer's ambition and a selector's prerogative. A cricketer has a right to play on until such time as he thinks he is fit and able and a selector has a right to determine whether that intent makes him worthy of a place in the team. You cannot barter a deal. That is for lesser pursuits in life, like being a member of Parliament before a no-confidence motion.

If, as in the current situation, you have players who have done very well for a long time and a call has to be taken on their future, the selectors first make up their mind

Before the Australia tour began, there was talk of phasing out four of the Fab Five—Ganguly, Dravid, Laxman and Kumble. There were also suggestions that the 'seniors' should retire on their own before they had to be dropped. By the end of the tour, Ganguly and Kumble did actually retire.

and then have a dignified conversation with the player concerned. The non-negotiable here is the selectors' decision. You cannot sign a deal with a player for four games, for example, and keep him in the side if he doesn't score a run in the first three and drop him if he makes a double hundred in the fourth.

Ideally that conversation should happen before a player's value has eroded but when the end is in sight. It should be a little nudge that says a push is round the corner. It then allows the player to either announce his retirement or take up the challenge and accept the push if the performance is not forthcoming. But for that to happen the selection committee has to be independent and their judgement non-negotiable. It is not impossible for it happens every day in places where merit is respected.

However, I fear that after a decent run, the selectors will struggle to explain some of their more recent actions. When we have a change in selectors, it is a touch unwise to use a broom and sweep everyone away because it is such a waste of knowledge acquired over a period of time. The old selection committee seemed to be working towards an end, which was to replace the ageing players in the squad. Accordingly a young man with promise, Rohit Sharma, was made the reserve player. But then, when his form slipped, he should have been in the Rest of India side to allow him to strengthen his case. Instead Mohammad Kaif was picked and that made him next in line. Remember Badrinath was picked after him. However, when the time comes to pick the national team, Badrinath jumps the queue. It is leaving a lot of people confused.

As it is with the Ganguly issue. Two days before this team was picked, Dilip Vengsarkar said that he wasn't physically fit enough to play at this level. Two days later, he presumably is. So, who is wrong? And therefore I have no clue about what the current policy with phasing out seniors is. The return of Ganguly is an admission of the fact that no youngster is knocking on the door loud enough to force the selectors to open it. Each of India's last six outstanding batsmen—Azharuddin, Tendulkar, Ganguly, Dravid, Laxman and Sehwag—did. You could argue that youngsters haven't been picked in the middle order for a long time now but you could, even more strongly, argue that they haven't done enough. I'd love to hear a national selector speak candidly about this.

Let's return then to where we began, to the VRS* story. If there is no such scheme, should it be flashed in the media? Indian cricket, or indeed anything to do with public life, will always spawn conspiracy theories. But a news channel, by its very nomenclature, tells the 'news'. It doesn't gossip, it cannot clothe conspiracy theories in holier garb because once it does so it no longer has the moral right to claim to be the 'news'. It worries me as well that more and more young men and women are getting obsessed with reporting what happens off the field rather than on it. And it doesn't help that the BCCI leaks more than a sieve. But should journalists be part of the 'leak', should they be mere mouthpieces?

Bright young men and women should love watching and reporting sport, not get increasingly drawn into the shenanigans that take place off the playing arena. If this is what we are telling the new generation about sports journalism, we are letting ourselves down. We are not leaving our profession in a better state than when we joined it.

---

*Voluntary Retirement Scheme.

CRICKET MUST GIVE IN TO REALITY

28 November 2008

England are right to go back. Cricket has to bow to reality. Anybody far away from home, however hospitable the conditions, needs to feel happy and wanted. You cannot live in an atmosphere of helplessness. If I was in a country where armed terrorists were searching for people who carry the same passport as I do, I would be on the next flight home.* Similarly India must not go to Pakistan† and I say so aware of how wonderfully hospitable the people of Pakistan have been in the past. But this is not about you and me, our views, our relationships. It is about sinister people.

It has been said that boycotting tours would play into

After the terrorist attack on Mumbai on 26 November 2008, England's one-day tour of India was cancelled and the England team flew back. They did, however, return to India to play the Test series.

*The terrorists in Mumbai were said to have specifically targeted foreigners.

†India's forthcoming tour of Pakistan was, expectedly, cancelled.

the hands of those that seek to disrupt; that playing on would be akin to thumbing our nose at them. But sportsmen have bats and hockey sticks, and sometimes just a quick pair of legs. They are entertainers. And even in our part of the world, cricket must grow insignificant at times. It is a game that brings a lot of joy and cheer and optimism, but it is just a game. It cannot compete with war. If you can, do tell me this is different; that this isn't war by another name.

What a pity though. Sport is one of the very very few things that can still unite people and bring a smile to the lips; that can help some of us forget reality, that can make us children again, delightfully impish and irrational. Maybe art can do that, and literature, and certainly music. But sport goes beyond. It invokes competition, it reminds us of who we are. We grow passionate and we compete and imagine we are sportsmen too. We score every run they do and take every wicket they do and smile sheepishly at our wives when we return the remote some hours later.

But in the end players go home, spectators do too, and we switch off our TV sets and go to bed; upset sometimes, disillusioned briefly, too, but we go home and we rise another day and we wait for the next game. Without sport we would be poorer, woefully poor, but in the hierarchy of needs it must cede place to safety, to comfort, to relief; to the thought that you will see your child the next morning. It must never be different, for some others are not so lucky. One day we may not be too, but until then our priorities must be in the right order. Sport should be played in an atmosphere of joy. You cannot make a painter paint with a gun to his head.

Our reputation has been dented. Visitors to our shores have been shot brazenly and our people too in trying to defend them. Sadly we are creatures of the environment we live in. If there is a drought in the jungle even the lion must leave. So too must we accept the times and the doctrines that surround us. As we benefit, so must we pay.

What a pity, because we are largely a hospitable people. We support our team and occasionally scream at the opposition; we challenge their way of living sometimes but we bestow great love and sometimes great luxury on them.

Hopefully this too shall pass.

As England head back they will be relieved and contemplative. They didn't play great cricket, certainly not as good as they can. If they look back dispassionately, they will realize they were outplayed in the big moments. They did threaten occasionally but seemed to accept too quickly that the going would be tough. They did themselves injustice. That is why I am so keen to see them play in the Tests. Hopefully things would have changed by then; the sea breeze would have taken this stench away and the Brabourne Stadium, such a wonderful home for cricket, will be packed and cheering.*

This morning, being with the family was comforting. Popping by to the other bedroom and seeing the boys sleeping calmly suddenly seemed so much more beautiful. It must be the same with everybody. That is why England had the right to make the decision they did. We must welcome them again—give them no quarter on the field, try to beat them, but welcome them to our land.

---

*The first Test against England, scheduled to be played in Mumbai, was subsequently shifted to Chennai.

THE GAME WE LOVE

4 March 2009

Like on far too many days in this part of the world, a bullet left this morning hoping to find a target. It did. In a cruel twist, it found people that carried guns, not those who cannot think beyond a cricket bat and a ball. There is huge relief at the fact that the Sri Lankan cricketers, the nicest, humblest cricketers in the world, survived; but let us not forget that those assigned to protect them died. Meanwhile, a rocket launcher missed its target, a grenade exploded after the team bus had passed over it, and cricketers scampered to the turf wicket at the Gaddafi Stadium—not to bowl a cricket ball or to face it but to escape in a military helicopter. This is the most recent portrait of the game we love.

Inevitably emotions will run high and hatred will fill the air. Responsible, elderly people will make whimsical,

---

A terrorist attack on the team bus carrying Sri Lankan cricketers in Lahore on 4 March 2009 injured several cricketers and led to the immediate cancellation of Sri Lanka's tour of Pakistan, and the blacklisting of Pakistan as a sporting venue until the security situation improved there.

dangerous statements and our game will be overwhelmed by those that speak another language. Neither emotion nor hatred is any good, nor, as we now know, is romance and naivety. Cricket's popularity has made it a target for terrible people and that is a fact, however depressing, that we must now live with.

I must confess that my heart goes out to the cricket lovers of Pakistan who are now faced with the prospect of not seeing any cricket for a very long time. There are a very large number of those who love the game with the same passion as Sundar from Chennai or Neel from Kolkata do. One of my greatest professional regrets is not being able to go to Pakistan on the 2004 tour, from which almost everybody returned with beautiful, almost magical, stories of the people they met and the warmth that was showered on them. Thereafter peddlers of hate seem to have taken over, and maybe I will now have to go to Birmingham or Melbourne to watch the game with Pakistani cricket-lovers—a sad by-product of our times.

Almost certainly there will be no World Cup in Pakistan.* Much can happen in two years but unless hatred, violence and terrorism are removed by some divine eraser I do not see anybody going to Pakistan. The mildest cricket team in the world has been attacked; people against whom you can have no animosity. There is no chance other teams will visit there. And sadly, it will have a deep impact on the future of cricket itself in that country.

For years, we in India have shifted our eyes westward, only marginally westward, with awe and admiration at the kind of talent that came bursting through. Suddenly Wasim Akram appeared, suddenly Waqar and Inzamam and Saeed

---

*The 2011 cricket World Cup was scheduled to be hosted jointly by India, Pakistan, Sri Lanka and Bangladesh.

Anwar and many others who, though not quite destined for greatness, played lovely cameo roles. In recent times that production line has got clogged. There is hardly any incandescent talent that illuminates stadiums now. And in the years to come it could only get worse. Wasim Akram was in awe of Imran, and Waqar wanted to be like him. Shoaib Akhtar wanted to bowl with Waqar . . . and that is how it always is. One generation inspires another, as Tendulkar did with Sehwag and Dhoni. If there is no cricket in Pakistan, there will be no inspiration. Expect lots of journeymen T20 players unsure of whether they are playing for Sussex or Northern Transvaal or South Australia.

This half-hour of madness in Lahore has far-reaching implications. Increasingly cricket grounds will be heavily guarded, cricketers will play in what look like garrisons; it will take longer to get into a T20 game than to actually watch it. Little children will no longer eye the wax paper packet in which their mother has packed the best sandwiches in the world. People might stay in drawing rooms, not only because they are more comfortable, but because they are safer. Increasingly cricket will be limited to what the camera shows and what the commentator says. If they can fight their way through all the advertising! I fear cricket-watching will become clinical rather than innocent.

Ultimately, though, cricket is only a tiny part of the reality of our existence. Like the movies, if more strongly, it can allow us to escape into our little cocoon for a few hours. But thereafter we must emerge and place it in the context of our times. This is a time of extraordinary hatred and violence, of tearing apart rather than stitching together; of grown-up men fighting like neighbourhood kids but with weapons that can maim and kill. The sad reality in our part of the world is that we have far too many people to police and far too few that don't need policing.

The ICC must act fast and not close their eyes to reality like they did with the Champions Trophy. A firm decision on the World Cup will have to be taken quickly and without emotion or appeasement. This is neither the time to cater to vote banks nor for the former gentry to get back at the nouveaux riches.

Oh, and by the way, there is another set of people attacking our game and they have struck thrice in two weeks: in Karachi, Antigua and Barbados where Test cricket was mauled by insensitive caretakers, producing the three most boring games you will ever see. While the ICC debates terrorism and the World Cup they will do well to come down strongly on those that destroy the game from within.

Until then let us mourn for the Pakistani policemen and count our blessings that Murali will continue to spin the ball viciously, that the great elegance of Jayawardene and Sangakkara will continue to grace cricket grounds, that Mendis will continue to mesmerize batsmen . . . indeed just that the Sri Lankans will play cricket.

SPIRIT OF CRICKET? IT'S NOW MERELY A STICK TO BEAT PEOPLE WITH

24 July 2009

Two captains, two very fine cricketers, Andrew Strauss and Ricky Ponting, are accusing each other of not playing according to the 'spirit of the game'. Hopefully, they know what they are saying because I don't, and I don't think anybody does. In truth, they sound as believable, as credible, as a starlet saying she did a nude scene because the 'script demanded it'.

We've been talking about this spirit of cricket thing for as long as I can remember. Every captain, when pushed into a corner, comes up with it. And yet, everybody, with no exception, violates one of the key clauses in the MCC's spirit of cricket declaration which the ICC has adopted. Point 5 says it is against the spirit of the game to 'indulge in cheating or any sharp practice, for instance:

The 2009 Ashes series was marked by harsh exchanges between the rival captains on whether the 'spirit of the game' was being followed.

255

(a) to appeal knowing that the batsman is not out.'

You probably see it twice every hour. In the Lord's Test one of the Australian batsmen, while swaying away, missed the ball by at least eight inches and it clipped the helmet on the way. Straightaway Matt Prior went up, you'd expect that, but so did Andrew Strauss at slip. Now if there were two people on the ground who knew for certain it wasn't an edge they were Prior and Strauss. Yet they were appealing vehemently for a catch and, by the sheer act of doing so, trying their best to induce an error from the umpire.

Ricky Ponting probably does it a couple of times a day himself and I'm not sure there is a player in world cricket who hasn't appealed convincingly knowing the batsman wasn't out. And yet, at the end of the first Test, Ponting told the media, 'We came to play by the rules and the spirit of the game. It's up to them to do what they want to do.' It staggers me. The spirit of the game is now merely a stick to beat people with and I'm afraid anyone who believes otherwise is being naive.

That is why you have to feel for the umpires who, at some times, have players appealing like they are auditioning for a part and, at others, have journalists and commentators like us peering at replays and looking for evidence to hang them. That is also why I read Rudi Koertzen's outburst with a touch of sympathy. Koertzen has had good days and bad days, like all of us do, but his explanation for his decisions on the two close catches at Lords was spot on. In one case, his colleague Billy Doctrove wasn't sure if the ball carried and so they referred it to the third umpire; in the other Doctrove was certain the catch had been taken clean and so he had no choice but to go with his colleague's judgement. That is what the law says. But Koertzen was roasted; you would have thought he'd just had dinner with Saddam and Osama.

It doesn't help matters that the rules of the game allow the umpires to use the replay to judge whether or not a catch was taken clean. The television replay will never be able to give a convincing verdict for a close catch. I thought we were done with all that. Indian viewers will remember the uproar over the Ganguly catch in the Sydney Test.* The replays were inconclusive and so we could arrive at the conclusion that our emotions and the match situation wanted us to, just as it allowed the Australian supporters to take a contrary stand. It is a piece of legislation that is inherently flawed; going to the replay gives you the feeling you are going to a superior court of appeal but the judge there is ruling on insufficient evidence.

You cannot go down the other path and take a fielder's word either. I'm afraid, in sport, nobody's word counts for much. Some cheat less than others, but nobody passes the acid test: appealing when they know the batsman is not out. And that is why, while batsmen are entitled to feel disappointed when a decision goes against them, we need to ask whether they ever did an opposition batsman in by misleading an umpire.

Eventually, therefore, it leads to the same conclusion. Use technology where it is as foolproof as it can get and, on other occasions, accept the umpire's word. The truth is that batsmen, bowlers, fielders, commentators and journalists make as many mistakes as umpires do. Or maybe even a couple more!

---

*In 2008

AS WE MOVE TO SHORTER FORMATS, THE NEED TO BE VIGILANT IS GREATER

7 August 2009

There is little doubt that drug testing has to be mandatory in cricket. Every good system must create an atmosphere for the clean to thrive and the weeds to be uprooted. There are both in our sport, as there will be even among priests and kindergarten teachers. Sometimes you don't just have to be clean, you have to be demonstrably clean, a small price to pay in the effort to cleanse a sport. Assuming this meets with universal approval, you have to accept that testing, like checking a cricket ball for tampering, has to be random and irregular. If the thief knows when the policemen are coming, he is unlikely to be pursuing his profession at that time!

Whispers about the intake of unusual substances have

The ICC announced in August 2009 that it would start random testing for drugs following the World Anti-Doping Agency's (WADA) guidelines. The BCCI was the only major cricketing board that refused to conform.

been going around in the cricket world for a while now. In a naive world you would put that down to mischief mongering but, while some whispers have remained whispers, others have been proved right. There was ball tampering, there are bookies, and matches, as we now know, have been subjected to differing degrees of influence. True, cricket probably doesn't need the extreme physical effort that track-and-field athletes and cyclists do (in the rogues gallery those are the prime portraits) but, as we move increasingly to a shorter form of the game, requiring concentrated but small bursts of performance, the need to be more vigilant is greater.

There is one point, though, in favour of what the cricketers have been saying. Given that cricket, unlike athletics or cycling, is not a seasonal sport, there is little time to retreat to an inaccessible place and pump yourself up. There is actually too little off-season training. Maybe one way out is to insist on random drug tests in bilateral tournaments as well, not merely those conducted by the ICC. And while we begin that process immediately we work out what is the best way to include randomness in testing. And if, thereafter, the method suggested by WADA emerges the best, so be it. There are many simple hardworking people who would happily agree to being subjected to a few random tests a year in return for so much.

Maybe there is something else we could do in parallel. It might be a good idea to tell our younger cricketers stories of athletes dropping dead in their twenties, of cyclists and sprinters and others who grew grotesque appendages and who exist in the obituary columns and jails rather than in medals tallies. Fear has always been a greater deterrent than force.

Meanwhile, Sachin Tendulkar, as clean a cricketer as

any you will meet, has gone public with the targets in his mind. I am intrigued because that is one thing he has never done in all these years. Yes, winning the World Cup is an ambition that everyone harbours and Tendulkar has made no secret of the fact that he yearns for it, but the fact that he has announced this target of fifteen thousand Test runs is unlike him. He needs another 2227 runs to get there and, even if he can retain an average of 50, it means another 45 innings. Over a long career he has averaged 1.64 innings per Test so it would be pretty safe to work with 27 Tests as the number he needs to play. I see two things coming in the way. First, his body needs to hold for that long and he has to maintain the resolve to go through more sets of rehab, something that gets increasingly difficult. Second, more critically, the BCCI needs to schedule 27 Tests quickly enough. My suspicion is that we are looking at a minimum of three years, three injury-free, good-form years. It is a daunting target and one that I will be overjoyed to see surpassed.

LIKE SUSPECT ACTIONS, BOARD SHOULD CRACK DOWN ON OVERAGE PLAYERS TOO

20 November 2009

So umpires in India have started calling bowlers for chucking—it is nice to see a forgotten law being implemented! Some bowlers, especially those who have played first-class cricket for eight or ten years, might choose to disagree with the current practice; they are entitled to be a bit confused, but really, in our part of the world, we had no alternative. In law, in spirit and in fairness, bowling has to be a straight-arm exercise; a definition that has been mutilated over the years. I suspect the reason umpires have started calling bowlers is not because during an off-season revision they discovered a law that seemed abandoned, or because they feel very strongly about it, but simply because there is now a list of offenders, and umpires have been given the freedom to call them. It is a welcome change.

At the beginning of the 2009 season, the BCCI instructed all umpires in first-class cricket to call bowlers for chucking.

Bowlers might complain that they were fine all this time and it is a bit unfair to call them now. But the law hasn't changed, merely the tools for its implementation. With fixed cameras at every first-class game, there is no place to hide any more and, in any case, the argument against unfairness suffers when confronted with the number of wickets they have obtained with illegal actions over the years. In truth it had become an epidemic (isn't it ironic that sometimes progression to epidemic status forces action to be taken?) and reached a stage where, if we saw a finger spinner, rather than see how good he was we were overjoyed that he actually bowled with a straight arm! That is exactly the feeling I had when I first saw Shakibul Hasan, the talented Bangladeshi cricketer. That he was a good bowler was almost secondary, that he didn't bend his arm was a surprise.

The idea of calling a bowler on the field is sound for at least a couple of reasons. The current procedure at the ICC is cumbersome and has an inbuilt failure mechanism. Umpires can only report bowlers, and, if they report them frequently enough (and they can keep bowling until then!), they have to, after remedial action, demonstrate the legality of their action before cameras in an artificial situation. That is easily done. Now, umpires are looking at what a bowler does in a tense, sometimes desperate, situation and that is the best indicator of how clean his action is at that moment. A bowler might bowl five clean deliveries and let one slip through. Only the on-field umpires can catch the moment.

India have actually done a commendable job by shortlisting bowlers with suspect actions, based on video footage, inviting them to the NCA for remedial action and warning them that future transgressions will invite a no-ball call from an umpire. Bowlers therefore, are aware that they are under the scanner and that, in effect, takes much of the sting out of their argument. Now, if everybody took care of this at the domestic level, we would have few problems at the international level where, currently, bowlers seem to enjoy greater latitude.

What this tells me is that intent is often the starting point, and therefore the stumbling block, for change. Intent has led to this action against one of the two epidemics in our cricket. Now we must look at the second—the problem with cricketers' ages. When I see the age against a player's name on some of the graphics, I cringe; it is embarrassing. In all fairness, once players are playing international cricket it shouldn't matter what number goes against their name in the age column, since it is one player's ability versus another. And irrespective of what a certificate says, the body knows its real age and so it knows when to send out the right signals. The problem is at the Under-19 levels where you see players of every vintage on the field.

So either we crack down on players very early, which is difficult because local administrators and doctors are pretty strong and willing accomplices, or we reduce the importance given to Under-19 cricket. Today, because of the attention, and the resultant monetary benefit, there is a temptation to stay nineteen for just a little while longer! It is unfair on genuine seventeen-year-olds because a two- or three-year age gap can be very large at that level.

I'm waiting to see a news report that says an Under-19 cricketer was banned for three years for being found overage.

GOOGLE DEAL MAKES GEOGRAPHICAL BOUNDARIES IRRELEVANT

22 January 2010

There was a time not so long ago when your address defined which cricket matches you could see. So as a kid growing up in Hyderabad we were thankful for what we got: a three-day game sometimes when, to our great joy, our school gave us a holiday to be able to go and watch. You had the radio of course but, as I later discovered, when a commentator knows his audience cannot watch what he is describing, he takes the odd liberty!

Then television arrived and, while that opened a beautiful new world for us cricket watchers, you could only see games that were beamed into your country; sometimes you only got the highlights but you were thankful for that. Our world was still bounded; what we saw was still controlled by someone else. Luckily, satellite television arrived and you could watch almost everything, provided of course, you had the time. One constraint had been removed—at the time we thought this was as good as it

---

In January 2010, the Indian Premier League announced a landmark deal that would enable Google India to stream live matches.

gets. But this week I heard something that's got me all excited because it makes the viewer king, something that was ingrained in me when I began a career in broadcasting.

What the IPL–Google deal does is to make geographical boundaries irrelevant in the area of live sport. So my classmate in Japan who was starved of his regular fix can now watch a game in real time as long as he has a workable broadband line—a problem that, unlike me, he doesn't need to worry about! It gets better. He can now access an online library free of cost. I recognized the value of that when I was trying to search for the amazing catch that Manish Pandey took in the final of the Ranji Trophy (by the way another example of a good pitch producing a good match). It was worth the search!

But, far beyond allowing people to watch cricket free of cost, I think it will also lead to a democratization of talent. If you are good, you can now prove it. Let me explain. When I was growing up, there was the subeditor in a newspaper who could, if he chose to, deny you an opportunity to appear in print. And, if he was benevolent, he would let you through, but could rewrite your article, even chop it and make it look quite different from what it was intended to be. The blog changed that; it gave talent the space it needed. You may not have had the reach but at least you had an outlet. It was empowering.

You can now do that with television content. With an online library, you can edit footage, store it in the manner you want and show that you can be smarter than the guy who edits for television. Better still, you can mute the commentary and put on your own and judge for yourself whether you are indeed better than the guys on television you are stuck with. It won't surprise me at all if that does indeed happen, since some of the best analysis I have read on cricket comes from blogs that intelligent people write. It is a revolution and it is round the corner.

THE WORLD IS CHANGING AND INDIA'S ECONOMIC MIGHT HAS TO BE ACCEPTED

2 July 2010

So cricket sits on the precipice again? Rabble-rousers and respected cricket writers are sharpening their phrases warning of the impact of a brown–white divide; there is talk of digging in heels and taking warlike positions. After a temporary lull the peace flags are down. Is it us and them all over again? I fear we overreact, blind to our failings, and discover pure venom in differing ideologies and cultures. I suspect we need to be a little more realistic, a little more understanding of the decisive way the world is changing.

Remember, we are a very small sport, no more than ten countries really and, with an inequitable distribution of

---

On 30 June 2010, the nomination of John Howard, the former Australian prime minister, to the post of ICC vice-president was rejected by six of the ICC's ten Test-playing members: India, Pakistan, Sri Lanka, Bangladesh, South Africa and the West Indies. England, Australia and New Zealand voted in favour while Zimbabwe abstained. New Zealand's Alan Isaac was later appointed vice-president.

wealth and opportunity, it is not very difficult for power blocs to emerge. The ICC is a very political organization, but so is every single sporting body from the IOC to FIFA. To believe otherwise is naive. It might seem, therefore, that on the surface Zimbabwe and South Africa led the opposition to John Howard but his nomination would not have failed without India's support. Ah, India again! That is where I believe the resentment lies. It is not surprising, for India is seen in some countries as a nouveau riche brat flexing his muscles at every opportunity.

India has stumbled onto leadership through a combination of demographics and an unshackled middle class. A country long seen to be tame and accepting is now being looked upon as devious and manipulative. That should surprise no one, because leaders around the world use their power to manipulate and to subjugate. It is not a worthy trait to possess, but India is neither the first nor will it be the last.

When they controlled the ICC, England were both condescending and manipulative. Having lost two series to India in 1971, at home, and in 1972–73 away, they forced through a temporary legislation restricting the number of fielders on the leg side to five, thus negating India's spinners. They regularly looked down at our part of the world and I have personally been at the receiving end of three instances of offensive and insulting behaviour at Lords. This is not to say the English are terrible and villainous—perish the thought—just that power makes certain people behave a certain way.

The closest similarity to the financial power India currently enjoys in cricket is that which the United States had over world politics post the Second World War. The United States openly took sides, openly protected its allies, created discord among those that dared stand up, funded rebellion and, through such manipulation, maintained its leadership position. Like with India, it was the financial muscle of their markets that was at the heart of it. We in India know that well from 1971 and the crippling financial sanctions because we thought we were mature enough to possess nuclear power.

The East India Company was manipulative, as were the Mughals who inflicted rather more gruesome ends on those that opposed them. Indeed, so were the Rajputs and the other princely states. Indian politicians are deeply manipulative, as were George Bush, Dick Cheney, Richard Nixon and Henry Kissinger, and I would venture to say it is almost an inevitable outcome of possessing power. And so India's cricket officials are currently flexing their muscles and, should the cycle change again, as it delightfully does, Australia will flex their muscles too. Don't think otherwise. Power tends to create tyrants out of perfectly reasonable people. Mandela and Gandhi were exceptions.

And yet, I would love it if India were different; if it could indeed take the lead in governance and transparency, focusing on making cricket a richer sport rather than dragging it through controversy. In recent times India has been in the news for annulling signed contracts; for being in dispute with the income tax authorities and other legal entities; every time the question of television rights comes up, it is accompanied by many battles in court. Conflict of interest and lack of transparency, though global features as we saw post Iraq, almost define Indian cricket. While many leaders are manipulative, the truly great are statesmanlike, and India have that opportunity—one they are currently squandering.

The message for the erstwhile rulers is that the world is changing. This is not a catcall of joy, merely an economic fact and I will be disappointed if it is misinterpreted. On

Thursday the CEO of HSBC Group said, '. . '. the shift from the West to the East is unstoppable . . . It starts in India and goes all the way down to Australia . . .' Cricket, a very tiny part of the world, merely mirrors that.

A group of ten cannot afford to be at war with each other; they cannot take up strident positions. There must be other ways. Acceptance and cooperation can open the doors to those.

WILLINGNESS TO EMBRACE INDIAN CULTURE: A PREREQUISITE FOR GARY'S SUCCESSOR

22 April 2011

So Gary Kirsten is back in Capetown, doubtless feeling like a bride in a swayamwar fending off suitors of varying pedigree and searching for the right one. Kirsten was very good but he was brave too. He knew what he wanted and was willing to sacrifice opportunity for it. Not all of us have priorities that are as clear, not all of us are selfless enough. Maybe that is why he made a good coach. We must wish him well and look for another.

But the position of India's cricket coach is not an easy one to fill because we are a landscape of the most diverse cultures existing within one country. We can bewilder easily, we are too heterogenous to understand. We pass legislation in favour of the gay community while we are home to people who murder their aunt on suspicion of

---

Gary Kirsten completed his tenure as coach of the Indian cricket team at the end of the 2011 World Cup. He was later appointed coach of the South African team.

being in a same-sex relationship! We accept hunger and give in to hunger strikes. Our young players come from poor families and grow exceedingly rich in very little time. Understanding India isn't easy, and yet that must be a primary requirement for the coach of the Indian cricket team.

And so, whoever it is that is finally appointed, must be willing to embrace our culture—not loan himself to it but marry into it. For if he is unwilling to do that, he will not understand the young men who play the game, the administrators who run it, the media that covers it incessantly and the people of India who smile and cry and, deep within, live and die with the sport. It is not about whether it is right or wrong—a coach cannot be judgemental about a culture—but about how it is.

You can have a fine candidate, but if he is reticent about accepting another culture, he is the wrong candidate. India can baffle and frustrate but can also love without limits. A South African was carried around the ground, to his visible embarrassment, by his young Indian wards as a sign of respect after the World Cup was won. Money and contracts don't buy that. The coach of the Indian cricket team is not a job; it is a relationship with some emoluments thrown in. It is not like coming to run the Indian operation of a multinational corporation.

We need to look for a man with an extraordinary work ethic, for that is not, inherently, the strength of Indian cricket. He must be willing to stay in the background, which will be a challenge because our media can be extremely intrusive. He must be a giver, it cannot be 'his' way and no other because with him will be cricketers who have their way, a way that has been successful. And he must be low-key because, before he realizes it, he can be caught in a political whirl. Indian cricket is not easy to understand and therefore we need to pick a man who does not seek to head down that path.

He has to be someone who has done it himself on a cricket ground because India, like no other nation, is unwilling to listen to someone who doesn't have a track record. Kirsten could have done everything else right but he would not have been accepted if he hadn't been a top Test player. India can never have a John Buchanan* or a Mickey Arthur.†

But, for some reason, India cannot have an Indian coach, and so we have to live with the fact that a new man will turn up every few years and take time to understand the country, its people and its cricket. It is something that Indian cricket, once it stops being obsessed with finances and power, needs to look at. India, or for that matter any Asian nation, seem to be pretty good at producing cricketers but not coaches. Indeed, of the ten IPL franchises, nine have overseas coaches. There must be a reason.

The generation that must coach today didn't earn as much as those they might coach. It is critical to understand, for they probably need the job and could be pliable, could be politically influenced. Many seek to forward their case through friends in the media, and will not be able to terminate that relationship or keep it at arm's length. If what happens in a selection committee meeting, for example, is routinely transmitted, surely what happens in a team meeting can be as well. Can players, then, share their deepest anxieties and fears with the coach?

---

*Immensely successful coach of the Australian team from 1999 to 2007, who never played a Test match himself.

†Coach of the South African team from 2005 to 2010, who also never played a Test himself.

While I would love to know what Yuvraj Singh went through or Sreesanth does, I find it reassuring in a way that I don't. I believe, though, that the players exiting the game now will be more at peace with themselves, and can become coaches in time to come. Surely a Kumble can, a Laxman can.

Hopefully Indian cricket will find a good man. But it is nice to know that the right man for a bigger job, the captain of the national team, already exists!

FLETCHER THE PERSON MORE IMPORTANT THAN FLETCHER THE TEACHER

29 April 2011

It is not always that a student recommends his teacher for a job. It can be tricky because the student, widely travelled and successful himself, may have acquired skills that actually make him better; and the halo he creates around his teacher may not be universally seen. But Gary Kirsten, who has been an honourable man, recommended Duncan Fletcher and the BCCI said 'Yes, we do'.

Though a coach neither scores runs nor takes wickets, Fletcher comes with an impressive track record and is widely respected by captains he has worked with. Nasser Hussain, a voice that the cricket world can trust, pays him huge compliments, and it is interesting that the only people who were less than effusive were those who were watching from more than a hundred yards away. As someone who

---

On 27 April 2011, Duncan Fletcher, former Zimbabwe captain and coach of the England team from 1999 to 2007, was appointed coach of the Indian cricket team, succeeding Gary Kirsten.

has been in residence in that suburb of a cricket ground for a long time, I can tell you that we do not always know the dynamics of what is afoot. I'd rather listen to a captain's or a player's view on a coach they have worked with than anyone else.

The challenge facing Fletcher is very different from that he faced when he had the job in England in 1999. England, then, had sunk as low as they could, and when that happens, self-belief and confidence can exit quite quickly. The only way, really, that England could go from there was up and Fletcher walked alongside two fine captains in Hussain and Michael Vaughan (who too pays him handsome tribute). Winning the Ashes in 2005 was English cricket's highest point for over twenty years, maybe more.

But now he comes to India, culturally and attitudinally very different, but also enjoying their best standing ever in the world game. India are a side full of confidence, but who need to sustain performance in a period that will also see a fairly epochal transition. Three of their best batsmen and their best bowler are in the latter stages of their career and a new generation is on its way. And it is a generation that has not been shaped by Ranji Trophy cricket but by 20- or 50-overs cricket. It is an extraordinarily rich generation with the bulk of the money having arrived through half-hour performances. They will need to be mentored through the longer form and that is where I believe Fletcher's greater role will lie: in being a father figure to a new generation of cricketers whom he must, very quickly, begin to understand.

This is a very different generation from any Fletcher might have seen. They, certainly the batsmen, are extraordinarily gifted, confident, even brash, and the subject of more adulation than in any other land. But they are mercurial and temperamental too, periods of excellence mingling with bouts of surprising barrenness. But Kirsten showed that a soft approach works very well with them; the how-can-I-help-you rather than the this-is-how-you-do-it approach. Eventually, when cricketing pedigree is unquestioned, it is the person you are rather than the knowledge you possess that determines success. That will be Fletcher's test: the person he is more important than the teacher he is.

He will discover too that in India it is important to be liked, to be seen as a 'nice' man as Sourav Ganguly frequently referred to John Wright in spite of their many disagreements. Many tough coaches around the world talk about how they are not there to be popular but to be effective. I believe that is fine for a leader, which is what the captain is, but not quite so for a mentor who must necessarily play the role of the caring elder, which is why my first reaction to the Fletcher appointment was that he must be able to embrace and understand a country and its people.

The good thing for Fletcher though is that India have a settled, and excellent, captain. Both Vaughan and Hussain have said that Fletcher made it clear that it was the captain's team at all times, and that in a disagreement over selection for example, the captain's word counted for more. Dhoni will like that because now, more than ever before, this is his team. Taking India to number one in the Test ranking was only the last leg of a relay that had started earlier, but winning the World Cup was about his team.

On paper, this is a good appointment, but what looks good on paper is merely the first step to success. As an old-time man-manager Duncan Fletcher will know that.

UDRS PROPOSAL GOOD IN THEORY

13 May 2011

The ICC has been doing some brainstorming and I am glad to see that the brain has won over the storm. The proposal to extend the use of the UDRS is good in theory but must remain free of complex 2.5-metre clauses that confound everyone. The equipment has to be uniform, which means budgets must be found, and those cannot come from the television-rights holder. And the integrity of the men and women manning the technology must, at all times, be above board because, in essence, the judge is now the technician rather than the umpire.

The suggestion to do away with the runner was probably inevitable but takes away a little bit of the gentlemanliness that once marked cricket. There was honour in winning fair and square rather than against an injured opponent,

In May 2011, the ICC called for the usage of the Umpire Decision Review System (UDRS), the implementation of which the BCCI had been opposed to, in all international matches. It also proposed to do away with runners, restrict the batting powerplay to between the 15th and 40th overs, and to use two white balls, one from each end, for each ODI innings.

but it was always going to be up against the deeds of sly
cricketers who misused the law. You can no longer have a
quaint thatched-roof dwelling in a steel-and-glass township.
If the runner does go, the players have to grin and bear it
because they were the cause. And now maybe we need
legislation against frivolous appealing. As long as it exists
nobody can ask that players be taken at their word.

The original purpose of the power plays, to drill some
enthusiasm into the middle overs, was not being achieved;
hence the suggestion that they be used only between overs
15 and 40. I will be interested to know what captains think
of it, though there are already some eminent ones in the
panel that recommended it. It might seem that the playing
conditions are intruding too much into the flow of a game,
but even the mandatory time-outs in a 20-over game are
slowly being accepted. It will mean that captains and
cricketers have to be even more versatile and quick on their
feet and that cannot be bad.

The game is being asked to take another look at a
concept that existed twenty years ago. Two white balls
were then used in a 50-over game in Australia and eventually
it was felt that the seamer had too much of an advantage
and that the spinner had too little to play with. By the time
a ball was 20 overs old you were, effectively, in the fortieth
over. But much has happened since. At the World Cup fast
bowlers often got a ball that the spinners had already used,
and in the IPL we are seeing that slow bowlers are now
quite adept at using the new ball. It might lead to peculiar
situations, though, where the ball might reverse more at
one end than at another, and certainly will not do so as
much as it now does. But at least the umpires will now be
obliged to take a look at it every over!

I hope the Cricket Committee's recommendations are
accepted because that is the reason the committee has been

constituted—to get the player's views. It is the best way forward for the game, the players work the playing side, the administrators the commercial side. It rarely works when those roles are interchanged!